PRAISE FOR *THE GREATEST ZOMBIE MOVIE EVER*

"A funny and spirited romp."

—*Kirkus Reviews*

"Fans of comical books rejoice as Strand has hit the zombie trend on its head with this one... Aspiring filmmakers, zombie movie fans, and reluctant readers should be entertained by this title."

—*School Library Journal*

"Readers will come away not only with stomachs aching from laughter but with the stars in their own eyes a little brighter for following Justin's rocky progress."

—*Booklist*

"[Strand] hits his stride with sarcastic conversation and the relationship dynamics. This novel will appeal to anyone trying to create something great against all odds—or anyone who needs a laugh."

—*RT Book Reviews*

PRAISE FOR *I HAVE A BAD FEELING ABOUT THIS*

"Fans of Strand's other novels of outrageous circumstance… will not be disappointed. A delightfully ludicrous read."
—*School Library Journal*

"Just the thing for teen wiseacres who don't mind a bucket or three of blood."
—*Booklist*

PRAISE FOR *A BAD DAY FOR VOODOO*

"Jeff Strand is the funniest writer in the game, and *A Bad Day for Voodoo* is wicked, wicked fun. Dark, devious, and delicious!"
—Jonathan Maberry, *New York Times* bestselling author of *Rot & Ruin* and *Flesh & Bone*

"Humor and horror collide in Strand's YA debut."
—*Publishers Weekly*

"For a reader intentionally seeking a wacky horror/comedy, this book delivers."
—*VOYA*

STRANGER
THINGS HAVE
HAPPENED

JEFF STRAND

sourcebooks
fire

Published by Sourcebooks Fire, an imprint of Sourcebooks, Inc.
P.O. Box 4410, Naperville, Illinois 60567-4410
(630) 961-3900
Fax: (630) 961-2168
www.sourcebooks.com

Library of Congress Cataloging-in-Publication data is on file with the publisher.

Source of Production: Versa Press, East Peoria, Illinois, United States
Date of Production: February 2017
Run Number: 5008560

Printed and bound in the United States of America.
VP 10 9 8 7 6 5 4 3 2 1

Dedicated to everyone who has asked or been asked:
"Is this your card?"

1

"IS *THIS YOUR* card?" asked Marcus Millian III, holding up the nine of hearts.

"It is!" said his mother, eyes wide with surprise. "How did you do that?"

Marcus sighed. "Seriously, Mom?"

"What's wrong?"

"That wasn't the card, and you know it."

"Well, true. But I didn't want you to feel bad."

Marcus grabbed his mother's hand and led her out of the kitchen into the dining room. The meatballs on her plate of spaghetti had been arranged to form the number two and a club.

"You were supposed to say no. Then I'd look all disappointed and say, 'Okay, I guess I need to practice the trick more.' And then we'd sit down for dinner, and you'd see your card number in the spaghetti."

"That's pretty clever."

"I can't become a master illusionist if you're just going to humor me. The magician is supposed to deceive the audience, not the other way around."

"You're right. You're right," Mom said.

"I'm fifteen. That's something you do with a six-year-old. I can take criticism. Do you think Penn & Teller's parents fibbed to them about it being the right card?"

"You've made your point. It won't happen again." Mom smiled. "Next time I'll throw the card down in disgust and say you're not my son. Go call your father for dinner."

Marcus had been testing a trick in which the picture frames on the wall in his father's office would rearrange themselves to spell "DINNER." It would require a fairly complex pattern of fishing line that he could manipulate from outside the room that he hadn't worked out yet, and there were only enough frames currently on the wall to form "DIN," but once it was perfected, he knew Dad would freak.

Until then, Marcus would have to resort to walking upstairs like a primate to pass along the message.

"Hey, Dad, dinner's ready," he said.

"Thanks." Dad saved the file he was working on, pushed back his chair, and stood up.

"Got time for a quick trick first?" Marcus asked.

"Of course."

Marcus shuffled his deck of cards, though it was a fake

shuffle that kept the two of clubs on top. His favorite card was the jack of diamonds, but the two of clubs was easier to construct out of meatballs.

"Cut the deck anywhere," Marcus instructed.

Dad cut the deck in half perfectly. Marcus frowned and furrowed his brow, pretending that the trick was ruined, and now it was going to be embarrassing and uncomfortable for everyone.

Misdirection—one of the most important skills for a magician.

Marcus set the two halves of the deck on the desk. "Look at the top card, but don't show it to me," said Marcus.

Dad complied, taking the card and glancing at it. He *thought* he was looking at the card where he'd cut the deck, but he was actually looking at the top card of the full deck.

"Stick it anywhere in the deck," said Marcus, and Dad slid the card back in.

Marcus did a full shuffle. "Would you like to shuffle it yourself too?" he asked. The order of the cards made no difference now, so he'd let Dad think he had more control over the outcome than he really did.

"Sure." Dad gave the cards a quick shuffle and then handed them back to Marcus.

Marcus stared at the deck, then pulled out a random card. The ace of spades. "Is *this* your card?"

"Nope."

Marcus feigned disappointment. "Are you sure you remembered it right?"

"Yep."

"Huh. Sorry. I guess I need to work on this trick some more."

"No big deal. It's all about practice," Dad said.

They went downstairs and sat at the dining room table.

"Looks great, sweetie," Dad said to Mom. He twirled some spaghetti on his fork, jabbed a meatball, and popped it into his mouth. "Delicious."

He quickly ate another bite. "So good."

He took a third bite. "Mmmmmm."

Marcus sat there stunned, staring as Dad had three more bites.

"What's the matter?" Dad asked. "Not hungry?"

"Did you notice the formation of your meatballs?"

"What?"

"You didn't look at them?"

Dad glanced down at his plate. "Is there something wrong with them? They tasted fine."

"They formed a two of clubs."

"Oh. Okay, yeah, no, I didn't notice that."

Marcus sighed.

"What? I don't analyze my dinner before I eat it!" Dad said. "You should have told me the magic trick was still going on! I would've paid more attention!"

"It was a simple card force. I wouldn't mess up a move that easy."

"How am I supposed to know how easy a trick is? That's between you and Grandpa Zachary."

Grandpa Zachary was actually Marcus's great-grandfather, who went by the stage name Zachary the Stupendous. Now eighty-nine years old, he'd retired twenty years ago and was mostly forgotten in the world of magic, but Marcus idolized the cranky old guy.

The two generations of Millians after Zachary had gone into respectable careers—teaching and nursing. Marcus had no intention of being respectable. He was going to bring the Millian name back into show business where it belonged.

If it were up to Marcus, he'd practice magic all day every day. Unfortunately, the law said that he had to go to school. At least he liked his teachers and studied hard. After all, the more he learned, the more material he'd have to create new tricks.

He loved close-up magic like card and coin tricks, but he wanted to create big, elaborate illusions that made people's jaws drop and their eyes bug out. And constructing those wasn't cheap. So he also mowed lawns in the neighborhood. Right now he was saving to buy some large mirrors that he wanted to use as part of a box he could climb into to make it look like he'd disappeared.

Since his family didn't own a riding lawn mower, his part-time job should have given him muscular arms. Sadly, thus far, muscles had eluded him. He was short and stick-thin, and he had curly red hair and freckles instead of the jet-black mane that would make him look more like a magician. He was working to grow a mustache and goatee without much success.

After dinner Marcus loaded the dishwasher. It would be a really cool trick to put dirty dishes in there, close the lid, open it up a few seconds later, and—*gasp!*—the dishes would be totally clean.

The original dishes would be covered with a thick layer of dried-on food. Maybe they'd even stink to better sell the illusion. When the dishwasher was full and he closed the lid, the rack would slide to the left, and a mechanism would replace it with an identical rack of clean dishes. This would involve cutting out both sides of the dishwasher and adding false sides that would fit perfectly when the second rack slid into position.

Of course, he couldn't actually perform this trick. Mom and Dad would not be okay with him cutting out large pieces of their dishwasher. He'd have to wait until he got his own place before he started destroying major appliances.

When the dishes were loaded and his homework was done, Marcus sat down at his desk with three plastic cups and three red balls. The trick was to make the balls disappear from one cup and reappear under another. Street performers often used this illusion to swindle tourists. The concept was simple, but it required quick sleight of hand and a lot of practice. He wasn't quite ready to show it to his friends yet.

Using the plural form of friend was probably inaccurate. More like one friend. Kimberly lived three houses down the street, and she enjoyed being his test audience. Yet oddly enough, she'd never said, "Since you're so good at magic, you should be my boyfriend!" Not that he'd ever tried to prod her in that direction, mostly for fear of messing up a perfectly good friendship.

And that was basically it for his social life—Kimberly and Grandpa Zachary.

Oh well. Marcus didn't mind. Much.

~~~~~

"What is this slop?" asked Grandpa Zachary.

"Shhhh," Mom hushed.

"Marcus, do your magic. Turn this food into something edible—wait. No magician has *that* much talent."

Marcus was with his family at a fund-raiser potluck for a local animal shelter. Since his retirement, Grandpa Zachary had focused his attention on raising money for charitable causes, although he had trouble sticking with any particular cause for very long. Last month he'd been saving the red-tailed hawk, which he later discovered was nowhere close to being an endangered species.

"I wouldn't feed this slop to the dogs we're trying to help," said Grandpa Zachary.

"Shhhh," Mom repeated.

"I'm speaking at a very low volume. The people who brought this vile gunk won't hear."

There were about fifty people in the park. Admission was five dollars. Plus you were supposed to bring your own dish of food to share. Grandpa Zachary didn't generate a lot of money for his causes, but he did give most of his free time.

Grandpa Zachary dipped a pretzel stick into the translucent goo and popped it into his mouth. "Actually, that's infinitely better than it looks. I withdraw my criticism." He snapped off the end of his pretzel so he wouldn't be accused of double dipping. (Grandpa Zachary *hated* double-dippers.) Then he plunged the pretzel into the sludge again. "Marcus Three, do me a favor. Find me a paper bowl so we can take this home with us. It's delicious."

Marcus went off in search of a bowl, grabbing an oatmeal raisin cookie along the way. The band, which had arrived half an hour late, was finally set up and ready to perform. The lead singer was wearing sweatpants, a white hat, and nothing else. He had dark circles under his eyes and looked like his latest shower was a distant memory.

"Good evening, everybody," the singer said into the microphone. He held onto the stand as if to keep himself upright. "We're Banjo Dan and the Wham Zaps. We've been drinking since nine-thirty this morning. Enjoy the show."

He plucked a few strings on his instrument, which Marcus was pretty sure was a ukulele and not a banjo.

"This is a benefit for an animal shelter, right? So here's a little song we wrote called 'Your Wife Is Uglier than a Dog.'"

"Nope, nope, nope, we won't be hearing that," said Grandpa Zachary, hurrying up to the stage. For an eighty-nine-year-old, the man could *move*.

Still, he wasn't fast enough to get there before Banjo Dan passed out. The other two members of the band just stood there, staring awkwardly at their fallen leader.

"What other songs do you know?" Grandpa Zachary asked them.

"Uhhhh…we actually just stand here and pretend to play."

"Begone!" cried Grandpa Zachary. "Take your snookered friend with you. Shame, shame, shame!"

The Wham Zaps dragged Banjo Dan away.

Grandpa Zachary picked up the microphone. "Ladies and gentlemen, I apologize for that crass spectacle. What a disgrace." He shook his head and started to scan the audience. "But the show will go on. Let us amuse you with a different act."

Marcus suddenly felt sick to his stomach. He began to sweat. It was hard to breathe. His feet hurt, even though he couldn't explain why.

Grandpa Zachary's gaze fell on him, and Marcus started to tremble. He loved to perform tricks for Kimberly. Loved to perform tricks for his great-grandfather. Loved to perform tricks for his parents. But he was *terrified* of performing in front of an audience. He'd never done it before.

It was a fear he knew he'd have to overcome to pursue his dream of being a famous magician, but he sure wasn't over it yet.

Grandpa Zachary cleared his throat. "Ladies and gentlemen, please put your hands together in a warm welcome for Marcus!"

2

MARCUS STARED AT Grandpa Zachary in horror. He wouldn't really call him up to the stage to perform a magic trick in front of fifty strangers, would he?

He shook his head a bit, hoping to telepathically convey his message of *NO NO NO NO NO NO NO!*

Grandpa Zachary smiled in a way that implied he had not received the message. "As most of you know, I used to be Zachary the Stupendous. How many of you like magic?"

Since Grandpa Zachary had not specified the method by which the audience was supposed to answer, people in the crowd raised their hands, applauded, cheered, and/or said, "Me!" A woman standing next to Marcus folded her arms in front of her chest and scowled.

"You there," said Grandpa Zachary, pointing to the woman. "Surely you enjoy magic!"

The woman shook her head.

"Why not?"

"I guess I'm just no fan of the devil."

"This isn't that kind of magic. I assure you no goats will be sacrificed here, especially since we're raising money for an animal shelter. The magic of which I speak is the art of *illusion*."

"Oh, that's okay then," said the woman.

"Ladies and gentlemen, everyone has to start somewhere. Before the great William Shakespeare wrote some of the most enduring works in the English language, he almost certainly wrote about a dolphin on the moon and spelled most of the words wrong. Before Alexander Graham Bell invented the telephone, he probably invented a prototype that burned your ear like a hot iron."

Marcus narrowed his eyes. He understood the point that his great-grandfather was trying to make, but he was making it very poorly.

Grandpa Zachary harrumphed. "I can see by the expression on a certain young man's face that my analogy is insulting instead of inspiring. So I present to you the first-ever public performance by the amazing, the astounding, the gobsmacking…Marcus Millian the third!"

"No, thank you," said Marcus.

"Don't be hesitant," said Grandpa Zachary. "Do you know what happens when you throw a non-swimmer into the ocean?"

"They drown?" asked Marcus.

"Nope."

"They get eaten by sharks?" someone else volunteered.

"Sometimes, but that's not where I'm going with this." Grandpa Zachary looked out into the audience. "Does anybody else have an answer?"

"The kid was right. They usually drown," said a man standing in the back. "It's a horrible way to go. Way worse than falling onto a pit of spikes. If you ever have the choice of how to die, go for the spikes. Trust me."

"Could we hear from somebody less ghoulish?" asked Grandpa Zachary.

A woman with an overflowing plate of peanut butter crackers raised her hand. "They learn to swim."

"Exactly!"

"Until they're pulled beneath the dark surface of the water by the jaws of a shark," the man interjected. "Sure, it's nice that they learned to swim so quickly, but that doesn't do you any good without arms or legs."

"Did you have a bad childhood?" Grandpa Zachary asked.

The man shrugged. "There were some rough patches."

Grandpa Zachary stared at him for a moment and then returned his attention to the rest of the audience. "My point was that in order to achieve greatness, sometimes we must face our fears before we think we're ready. And so, I present to you a beguiling illusion by the awe-inspiring, gasp-inducing prodigy...Marcus Millian the third!"

The audience applauded politely. Marcus stood there, motionless, as if his entire body had been covered with shellac.

"I didn't bring my cards," he said.

"Nonsense," said Grandpa Zachary. "You always carry a deck of cards. I can see card-shaped bulges in your pockets right now."

Marcus knew that he had two options. One, he could drop to the floor, curl into the fetal position, close his eyes, cover his ears, and let out a high-pitched shriek until everybody became so uncomfortable that they vacated the premises. Or two, he could go onstage and do a trick.

Option one sounded very appealing.

Nah, he'd just do a trick.

The audience applauded again as Marcus walked to his doom. "You'll do great, I promise," said Grandpa Zachary, handing him the microphone with a wink.

"Hello," said Marcus. "For my first trick, I will make my great-grandfather disappear."

Marcus waved him away, and Grandpa Zachary walked back into the audience as everybody laughed. Maybe performing for an audience wouldn't be so bad. It might even be fun. It was what he'd always wanted, right? He could do this. Move over, David Blaine. Marcus Millian III would amaze them all!

"I'm going to need a volunteer," he said.

"Me! Me!" said a little boy, waving his hand so frantically

that Marcus worried that it might fly off and hit somebody. "Me! Me! Me! Me! *Mememe!* Me!"

Marcus didn't really want to do this trick with such a young volunteer, but the crowd immediately went, "*Awwwww*," so Marcus didn't really have a choice without disappointing the crowd.

"Come on up here," said Marcus, wondering how much sweat weight he'd lost in the past ninety seconds.

The little boy ran over to him.

"What's your name?" asked Marcus. He held the microphone to the little boy's mouth.

"Donnie. I'm five."

"Nice to meet you, Donnie."

"I'm five." Donnie pretended to take a bite out of the microphone.

"What do you do for a living, Donnie?" Marcus asked. The audience chuckled.

Donnie turned toward the audience, his face red with fury. "*Don't laugh at me!*"

Marcus placed a comforting hand on the boy's shoulder. "It's okay, Donnie. They were just laughing at my joke."

"I'm five."

Marcus took a deck of cards out of his pocket. His fingers were trembling too badly for him to do one of his truly impressive shuffles, so he just did an old-fashioned riffle shuffle. "It's good you remember how old you are, Donnie. Are you good at remembering cards too?"

"I have a gerbil," Donnie said proudly.

"What's your gerbil's name?"

"Super-Gerbil."

"It's not your gerbil!" a girl in the audience insisted. "Mom, Donnie keeps saying that Super-Gerbil is his gerbil, but Aunt Maggie gave it to me!"

The girl's mother whispered something to her, and she stood there, glaring and quietly pouting.

Marcus fanned the deck of cards and held it out to Donnie. "Pick a card, any one you want. Don't show it to me."

"Can I keep it?"

"No."

Donnie took a card and then took another.

"That's two cards."

Donnie pretended to eat one of them. The audience chuckled. Marcus wiped the sweat from his brow with the back of his hand.

"Look at one of the cards and remember it," said Marcus.

"Okay."

"Now put the card back into the deck."

"Why?" Donnie asked.

"Because that's the trick."

Donnie licked one of the cards and giggled as he slid it into the deck.

"Please don't lick my cards."

"Why not?"

"Because they're covered in poison."

Donnie's eyes widened. It looked as if he might start to cry. Marcus realized that it wasn't a good joke to make to a five-year-old, and he'd suddenly become a villain in the eyes of the audience. Marcus wanted to astound the audience with his illusions, not his ability to reduce a young child to tears.

"Snot," he said quickly. "I meant it's snot."

Donnie licked the card again. The audience tittered. And Marcus continued to sweat.

Marcus glanced over at Grandpa Zachary, who gave him an enthusiastic thumbs-up. Marcus loved his great-grandfather, but he was going to say some unkind things to the old man when this nightmare was over.

"Okay, Donnie," said Marcus, "I'm going to need you to remember that card and put it back into the deck."

"It's sticky."

The audience chuckled again.

"*I said don't laugh at me!*"

"They're not laughing at you, sweetheart," Donnie's mother said. "They're celebrating you."

Donnie stuck the card back into the deck. Marcus began to shuffle. The trick would be less impressive to the audience now that the card was covered with saliva, but there was nothing he could do about that.

"What I need you to do, Donnie, is concentrate on the

card you chose. Concentrate as hard as you can. Picture it in your mind. Are you thinking about it?"

Donnie shook his head.

"What are you thinking about?"

"Pickles."

"Can you think about pickles in the shape of the card you chose? That's what I want you to do, Donnie. Imagine a whole bunch of dill pickles—"

"Ew! Dill pickles are gross!"

"Imagine a whole bunch of sweet pickles—"

"Ew! Sweet pickles are gross!"

"What kind of pickles do you like?"

"The ones at McDonald's."

"Those are dill pickles," said Marcus.

"*They are not!*"

"Focus, Donnie. Think about your card." Marcus needed to get this trick over with before it completely crashed and burned. His hands were still trembling, but this next step involved dexterity. He pocketed the deck and held up one card. "Donnie, how many cards are in my hand?"

"One."

"How many cards are in your head?"

"Huh?"

Marcus gave Donnie's ear a gentle tap. A stream of fifty-two playing cards cascaded out of the other side of his head, landing on the ground. The audience gasped and applauded.

"Are there any more in there?" Marcus asked. He tapped Donnie's other ear, and another stream of cards flew out the opposite side.

Marcus held up the single card in his hand, turning it sideways to show the audience it was just one card. One last tap on Donnie's ear, and an even longer stream of cards, 104 of them, shot out of the little kid's head. (Well, not really. It was a trick.)

"Thank you, Donnie!" said Marcus to the bewildered child as the audience applauded. "And thank you all for being here!"

He'd done it! Marcus had successfully performed a magic trick in front of an audience! And even with the Donnie-related challenges, he hadn't completely messed it up! He felt…well, he felt sick to his stomach, but not quite as queasy as he would've expected. Maybe if he kept this up, he'd feel less and less sick to his stomach with each subsequent performance until one day his gastrointestinal distress would be gone forever!

Oh, Marcus was still mad at Grandpa Zachary for volunteering him to perform. There were plenty of dirty looks left to give today. But aside from having Donnie's DNA on his card, Marcus was glad he'd done it.

The people in the crowd went back to socializing amongst themselves, apparently not upset that the event's replacement entertainment had consisted of one magic trick. Marcus didn't think anyone had been all that excited about Banjo Dan and the Wham Zaps in the first place.

"A fine job," said Grandpa Zachary, walking over and

shaking Marcus's hand. "A lesser magician would have stood there, slack-jawed, but not you. I'm proud of you. You are destined to become one of the all-time greats."

Somebody snorted.

Grandpa Zachary turned to face a large man in a dark blue suit. The man looked about fifty years old, with slicked back hair and chubby cheeks. Though the fellow was not setting hundred-dollar bills on fire in a grand display of pyrotechnics, he looked like he could without missing any of them.

"Good afternoon, Bernard," said Grandpa Zachary. The words were thick with disdain, as if he were addressing raw sewage bubbling up from the ground.

"Hello, Zachary."

"Haven't seen you in a while, for which I'm grateful."

"My theater keeps me busy."

"Why did you make that snorting sound?" Grandpa Zachary asked.

Bernard shrugged. "The boy's performance was okay. Nothing special."

Uh-oh, thought Marcus. He didn't really care that the guy insulted him, but Grandpa Zachary wouldn't stand for it. This was going to be very…interesting.

3

"HOW DARE YOU?" Grandpa Zachary said. "How dare you pollute the air between us with such ill-chosen words?"

"The kid has talent," said Bernard. "He's got a long and successful future ahead of him, performing at *birthday parties*."

Grandpa Zachary's eyes widened with fury. "You despicable wretch! I'd punch you in the face if we weren't raising money for puppies and kittens!"

"Calm down, Grandpa," said Marcus. "I'm all right."

"I'll not allow a man of such dubious moral character to disrespect you. Bernard Pinther isn't qualified to judge the freshness of a carton of milk, much less an artistic performance. Begone, foul cretin! Begone!"

Bernard sneered. "Maybe the boy should make me vanish."

"If he did, you wouldn't come back, I assure you!"

"Is that a threat?"

"Yes, but it's an empty threat. The boy's a talented illusionist, but he's not going to magically transport you into an alternate dimension from which there is no return. Grow up, Bernard."

"Ah, Zachary. You'll never change. You were overrated in what little there was of your prime, and now you're nothing but a bitter, old, washed-up has-been."

"Come on, Grandpa," said Marcus, trying to lead Grandpa Zachary away from a confrontation. "Let's go get some more of that delicious ooze."

Grandpa Zachary didn't remove his angry gaze from Bernard. "I'm not washed-up. I'm retired. There's a significant difference, as you would know if you understood how vocabulary works. And I'd like you to apologize to my great-grandson."

"Actually, I will," said Bernard. "He has no control over his ancestry. Marcus, I'm sorry for my rude comment."

Grandpa Zachary looked surprised and perhaps a bit disappointed. "Okay, good. Accept his apology, Marcus."

"I accept it," said Marcus, wishing he were in any of the trillions of other available places in the world than here.

"Now find somewhere else to stand and snort," Grandpa Zachary told Bernard.

Bernard nodded at Marcus. "Good luck to you, and be sure you learn how to make balloon animals."

Grandpa Zachary's rage returned. "How dare you apologize to my great-grandson and then use the same insult again?"

"It wasn't the same," said Bernard. "It was a variation on a theme."

"Marcus, withdraw your acceptance of his apology!"

"It's fine, Grandpa. I don't care what he says."

"Withdraw it!"

Marcus looked at Bernard. "I, uh, guess I take back accepting your apology."

"That's all right," said Bernard. "It wasn't sincere."

Grandpa Zachary gestured to Marcus. "Fetch me my boxing gloves from the trunk of the car! There's going to be a tussle!"

"Do you really have boxing gloves in your car?" Marcus asked.

"Of course I do! For just such an occasion! Hurry…before he flees!"

"I don't think Mom and Dad would like you fighting." Marcus looked around to see if his parents were watching what was happening. No, they were talking to the Hendersons, who seemed to be congratulating them on what a superb job Marcus had done. Or possibly they were exchanging zucchini bread recipes. Marcus couldn't tell.

"Five or six punches, and he'll be on the ground, writhing in pain! Get the gloves!" shouted Grandpa Zachary. "Fighting bare-fisted would be too dangerous. I can't risk having his death on my conscience."

Bernard chuckled. "Now, now, there's no need to resort to

physical violence. Marcus, I should not have made the balloon animal comment. It was inappropriate of me. I'm sorry."

"Should I accept that apology?" Marcus asked Grandpa Zachary.

"Absolutely not! Spit in his face!"

"I'm not going to do that, Grandpa."

"Good. It's never appropriate to spit in someone's face. That was a test. I would have been happy if you failed, but still, it would have been wrong."

"Sir," said Marcus to Bernard, "I think we can all agree that this conversation isn't going very well. I have to ask you to leave my grandpa alone."

"Fair enough. Again, I apologize. I'm only trying to look out for your future. To make up for it, I'll give you a useful piece of advice. When you negotiate the contract, make sure they're required to save you a piece of birthday cake."

Grandpa Zachary looked like his head was going to start shooting flames like a Roman candle. "Marcus, fetch me my machete!"

"Let's go, Grandpa."

"I've changed my mind! Fetch me a chainsaw! You've got a chainsaw in your garage, right? I'll keep him here while you go get it! Make sure it has plenty of gas!"

Now others were starting to stare. Which was embarrassing, but also nice because there'd be plenty of people to intervene if Grandpa Zachary really did throw a punch.

"I don't understand why you're so upset," said Bernard, clearly enjoying the whole scene. "It was just one tiny little snort."

"Marcus Millian III will be one of the greatest magicians who ever lived," said Grandpa Zachary, speaking to the entire crowd. "He's currently perfecting a bewildering illusion that will shock, stun, and astonish all of you! An illusion unlike anything the world has ever seen!"

Huh? Was he talking about the dishwasher thing? Marcus wondered.

"Mark my words, Bernard. You'll eat your words! You'll eat your words with liver and onions! This magic trick will melt your underused brain! The collective gasp from the audience will generate hurricane-force winds! When my great-grandson takes his final bow, not one pair of pants in the entire auditorium will be un-pooped!"

He definitely wasn't talking about the dishwasher trick.

"Is that so?" asked Bernard. "Would you like to place a wager on that?"

"I would indeed."

"How about ten thousand dollars?"

"No, we wager for the only thing that matters in this world—honor!"

"How about honor plus ten thousand dollars?" Bernard suggested.

Grandpa Zachary shook his head, which was a relief,

because Marcus knew he didn't personally have ten thousand dollars to wager.

"Of course a scoundrel like you places such a low value on honor. To me, it's enough. It's everything. And I am so confident in Marcus Millian III's prowess that I will put my own honor on the line."

"I don't get how it works though," said Bernard. "I mean, how does the transfer of honor happen?"

"It's an abstract concept. Just go with it."

"So when will this amazing illusion be ready?"

"Six weeks."

Marcus wanted to say something, like "*Noooooooooo,*" but his mouth wasn't working.

"I'll have to check my schedule, but why don't you take eight," said Bernard. "I should have a free afternoon by then for the Amazing Marcus to mystify us all."

"You don't get to pick his stage name," said Grandpa Zachary.

"I wasn't trying to."

"The Amazing Marcus has a nice ring to it, but now you've gone and polluted it."

Bernard stuck out his hand. "Do we have a bet?"

Grandpa Zachary shook it. "We do."

Marcus wanted to add something like "Hey, so, uh, do I get any say in this? I feel like I should have at least a little bit of say, and if you really think about what's happening here, you'd probably come to the conclusion that I should have the most say out of anyone since I'm the one most directly impacted by the discussion that's taking place right in front of me." But his mouth still wasn't working.

"Good luck to you both. I'll be in touch," said Bernard, and he walked away.

"That worm," said Grandpa Zachary. "No, he's what you would get if you crossed a worm and a rat. Do you know anybody who likes rats? Even other rats only barely tolerate them. That man is a loathsome worm-rat, and I look forward to humiliating him."

"I can't help but feel that you two have some sort of history," said Marcus.

"Yes. A long, ugly history. He's easily one of my top ten enemies. In fact, if Sinister Seamus hadn't survived the whaling accident, Bernard Pinther might take the number-one spot."

"I wish you hadn't made that bet."

Grandpa Zachary held up his hand. "It'll be fine. Hey, look at that. My fingers are trembling with anger. I haven't been this mad in a long time. It's kind of refreshing. I can see why the Incredible Hulk enjoys it so much."

Marcus lowered his voice so nobody else could hear him, even though people had long since stopped paying attention. "I'm working on tricks, but nothing like what you described. I can't deliver what you promised. You're going to lose the bet."

"Nonsense! You have Zachary the Stupendous on your

side. First thing tomorrow morning, you're coming over to my apartment, and we'll get to work."

"I have to go to school tomorrow, Grandpa."

"First thing tomorrow after school, you're coming over to my apartment, and we'll get to work."

"I have to mow four lawns after school."

"Don't they have robots to do that?"

"Not yet."

Grandpa Zachary frowned. "First thing tomorrow after you mow those lawns, you're coming over to—wait, will you have homework?"

"Yeah."

"I guess you should do your homework. So school, lawns, and homework. But no time for television, team sports, or girls. We've got work to do!"

"Can't you just cancel the bet?" asked Marcus. "I'd love to work on a bewildering illusion that will shock, stun, and astonish everybody, but I'd rather do it under less scary circumstances."

"He scoffed at your accomplishment. Nobody scoffs at a Millian and lives to tell the tale!"

"What?"

"That was an exaggeration, of course. I just mean that he'll be *emotionally* destroyed."

"I have a bad feeling about this."

Grandpa Zachary placed his hand on Marcus's shoulder. "I'm not going to pretend this wager wasn't encouraged by resentment and a short temper. But I also believe in you. I wouldn't put my honor on the line if I didn't think you could do this. You have the talent, Marcus. You have the creativity and the passion. When I said that you could be one of the all-time greats, that wasn't to annoy Bernard. I meant it."

Marcus smiled. "Thanks, Grandpa."

Donnie walked over to them. "I'm five."

~~~~

As Marcus lay in bed that night, his stomach felt as if it were filled with butterflies on energy drinks. He was excited about what he might accomplish. If he could do a trick in front of fifty people, why not fifty thousand? Why not fifty million? Or fifty-*one* million?

With Grandpa Zachary helping him, he could do this. He could indeed create and perform an illusion that would make everybody scream, "*Aaaaiiieee! Burn the warlock!*"

It was going to be awesome. Bernard Pinther being a jerk may have been the best thing to ever happen to Marcus Millian III.

~~~~

Marcus finally fell asleep but woke up to the sound of his mother crying. It was 3:17 a.m.

He got out of bed to see what was wrong. Mom and Dad were in the living room, sitting on the couch. Mom was on her cell phone, but Dad waved for him to come over and sit next to them.

Before they even said anything, Marcus had a horrible, unexplainable feeling that he knew why Mom was crying—Grandpa Zachary had died.

4

FOURTEEN YEARS AGO

Zachary reached for one-year-old Marcus's ear and then held up a shiny quarter.

"Look at this!" Zachary said as Marcus giggled. "His head is filled with cash! How much do you think we can get out of him?"

"Hopefully enough to pay for all of these diapers," said Marcus's mom. "Ugh. I think he needs changed again."

"And for my next trick, I'll make myself disappear!"

THIRTEEN YEARS AGO

"Grandpa, he's way too young to learn card tricks," said Marcus's mom.

"Nonsense. You're never too young to start learning the art

of magic. He needs to get used to the feel of cards. Sleight of hand takes years of practice, but he'll be the most talented illusionist in day care."

"Or he'll become a professional poker player."

"Good. He can win all of the other kids' juice boxes."

～～

TWELVE YEARS AGO

"That top hat is way too big for him," said Marcus's dad.

"Because it covers his entire head?"

"I can't see," said Marcus.

"His head just needs to grow," said Grandpa Zachary. "I think everybody here agrees that Marcus's head will continue to grow as he gets older. That's what heads do. Otherwise, he'll become a fully grown boy with a teeny tiny head, and he'll have much worse problems in life than just a hat that doesn't fit."

"Or we could exchange the hat," Marcus's mother suggested.

"No, it's like returning food at a restaurant. If you take a hat back, the cashier spits in the new one."

"I don't think that's true," Marcus's dad said.

Grandpa Zachary removed the hat. "Marcus, you've got some head-growing to do. I need you to close your eyes, put your fingers in your ears, hold your breath, and *push* as hard as you can."

"Don't do that, Marcus! Grandpa is just teasing," said Marcus's mother.

"Yes, I am." Grandpa Zachary winked at Marcus. "I've got a smaller hat in the other bag."

~~~

ELEVEN YEARS AGO

"Marcus, did I ever tell you that when I was fourteen years old, I ran away to join the circus?"

"*What?*" Marcus scooted up on Grandpa Zachary's lap.

"That's right."

"Did you see elephants?"

"I saw more elephants than you can shake a stick at. Big elephants, small elephants…well, they're all big, but baby elephants are smaller than grown-up elephants. I once saw an elephant smack a clown with its trunk. That was one angry clown, believe me."

"Did you see panda bears?"

"There were no pandas at this circus, but they did have bears. Big brown ones. And lions…and chimpanzees…and jugglers…and tightrope walkers…and a lady who looked like a lizard."

"Wow!" Marcus was always amazed and transfixed by Grandpa Zachary's stories.

"You're too young now, but when you're seven years old,

we're going to run away with the circus together. How does that sound?"

"Hooray!"

～～～

TEN YEARS AGO

"Marcus, don't ever do this trick at home, okay?"

"Okay," said Marcus.

"You promise?"

"I promise."

Grandpa Zachary reached for the napkin that was under his full glass of root beer…and yanked the napkin away. The glass didn't move.

～～～

"I'll pay to have the carpet cleaned, of course."

"It's okay, Grandpa," said Marcus's mom.

"I should never have shown him that trick."

"It's fine," she said.

"Children should drink more water and less grape juice anyway."

"Quit while you're behind, Grandpa."

～～～

NINE YEARS AGO

"Is this your card, Grandpa?"

"Nope."

"Is this your card?"

"Nope."

"Is this your card?"

"Nope."

"Is this your card?"

"Nope."

Twenty-eight cards later, it was.

~~~~

EIGHT YEARS AGO

Grandpa Zachary walked through the front door, holding a colorfully wrapped box. Marcus was sitting on the couch, crying.

"What's wrong with the poor boy? Nobody should cry on his birthday! That's unacceptable! Your first twenty-nine birthdays are happy occasions!"

Marcus's mom and dad looked kind of annoyed. Grandpa Zachary set the present on the table.

"Why don't you ask him what's wrong?" suggested Marcus's mom.

Grandpa Zachary sat down on the couch. "What spoiled your birthday?"

"Mom and Dad say we're not running away to the circus!"

"What?" Grandpa Zachary looked puzzled.

"You said that when I turned seven, we'd run away to join the circus."

"Oh." Grandpa Zachary shifted uncomfortably on the cushion. "How did you remember that? You were four."

"I remember!"

Grandpa Zachary looked over at Marcus's mom and dad. "This child is a genius. I can assure you that when I was seven, I didn't remember anything that was said to me when I was four. His brain must be abnormally large. I knew the head-growing exercises would be good for him."

"Mm-hmm," said Marcus's mom.

Grandpa Zachary turned his attention back to Marcus. "There aren't any decent circuses to join right now. But when you turn eight—"

"Grandpa Zachary!" said Marcus's mom in the same tone of voice she used when addressing Marcus by his full name.

"I made up the story about joining the circus," Grandpa Zachary admitted. "I would never take you away from your mom and dad to be part of a smelly circus. I should never have said that. I didn't run away until I was sixteen. So you'll just have to be patient for nine more years—"

Marcus's mom cleared her throat.

"What I mean is…wait until you graduate from high school—"

She cleared her throat again.

"When you graduate from college, then we'll run away to the circus together. I promise. Okay?"

Marcus wiped some tears from his eyes and smiled. "Okay."

~~~

SEVEN YEARS AGO

"Is this your card, Grandpa?"

"Nope."

"Is this your card?"

"Nope."

"Is this your card?"

"It is! Good job, boy!"

~~~

SIX YEARS AGO

"You hold the four corners of the handkerchief together. No, see, when you do it like that, the hidden flap isn't open. Here, let me move it just a bit. Yes, like that. Now if I'm standing right here, I can see exactly what flimflam is going on, so you need to be aware of your audience." Grandpa Zachary sat down in his recliner. "From this perspective, I will be absolutely mystified."

Marcus nodded.

"Let's try it from the top. Hold up the empty handkerchief."

Marcus held up the handkerchief by the top two corners, showing that it was without question a perfectly normal handkerchief that in no way varied from the handkerchiefs that normal people used to blow their normal noses on any normal day.

"Ask me for a coin."

"I now need to borrow a coin from somebody in the audience," said Marcus.

Grandpa Zachary reached into his pocket and held out a penny. "Say your line."

"That's very kind of you, sir, but magic is more exciting with real money at stake. Does anybody have a quarter or a silver dollar?"

"Perfect." Grandpa Zachary handed Marcus a quarter. "Bunch the handkerchief into a sack."

Marcus held the handkerchief by all four corners. "I will now make your hard-earned quarter…disappear!" He dropped the quarter into the sack, making sure it went into the hidden flap, and then released the bottom two corners. The handkerchief fell open, and the quarter was gone.

"Holy cow on a Popsicle stick!" said Grandpa Zachary. "It's vanished into the netherworld!"

"Can I keep the quarter?" asked Marcus.

"In your dreams. Let's try it ten more times before we show your mom and dad. You can keep their quarters."

~~~

FIVE YEARS AGO

"So how long are you grounded?"

"Two weeks."

Grandpa Zachary whistled. "That's brutal."

"Yeah. I don't get to go to the carnival and see the giant pig and the fire-eaters."

"Do you understand why it upset your mother when you pretended to pop your eyeball out?"

"Yeah."

"We make important choices in life. We must weigh our decisions against the possible consequences. When you pretended to pop out your eyeball, you knew you were going to get in trouble, right?"

"I guess."

"The reward for your action was that you got to hear your mom scream at the top of her lungs when she thought you knocked your own eyeball right out of your head. Then you got to hear her scream again when you popped it into your mouth. You got a lot of value out of that. In two weeks you won't remember what you missed when you were grounded, but you'll remember the glory of that moment for the rest of your life. I've got to be honest with you. I think you're getting a pretty fair deal."

Marcus shrugged. "Maybe." He'd been looking forward to seeing the fire-eaters for weeks.

"It's important that you accept your punishment. You deserve this grounding. You made your dear, sweet mother believe she had a one-eyed son. So I expect you to accept the consequences without whining, complaining, or trying to get her to change her mind. And as you sit up here in your dark, lonely room, remember the joy of a well-executed magic trick and how it was worth it."

"Thanks, Grandpa." Marcus had to admit that he felt a little better.

"And don't use so much ketchup next time. That's just gross."

~~~~

FOUR YEARS AGO

"Is this your card, Grandpa?"

Grandpa Zachary beamed. "Yes, indeed!"

~~~~

THREE YEARS AGO

"It's okay, Marcus. We've all thrown up at school. Nothing to be ashamed of."

"Sure it is! Everybody was laughing at me!"

"That's because it's delightfully amusing to watch somebody regurgitate." Grandpa Zachary grinned. "I'm just kidding. When they laugh, it's nothing against you. What they're really saying is, 'Thank goodness it wasn't me!'"

"I know! But it *was* me! Mrs. Pollert asked me to go up in front of the class and do my book report, and I just… I don't know. I just got so nervous that I felt like I was gonna throw up. And then I did."

"Why were you so nervous? You've talked in front of the class before, right?"

"Lots of times. I've always felt kind of sick when I had to do math problems at the board or give reports or whatever, but it's never been this bad. And it'll be even worse the next time because I'll know that I really *could* throw up in front of everybody."

"Being anxious is normal. When I used to do magic shows, I was always anxious beforehand. No matter how much I practiced, I was always worried that this would be the performance where I made a mistake. And sometimes it was. I wasn't a flawless magician. But you have to think, *What's the worst that can happen?*"

Marcus groaned. "I throw up in front of everybody."

"No, the worst would be wetting your pants. But those years are behind you. Look, the other kids will make fun of you for losing your lunch. It's inevitable. They may even give you a nickname to mark the occasion. Something like…hmmm, are there any synonyms for vomit that start with the letter M?"

"I'm not sure," said Marcus. "I can't think of any."

"There has to be at least one. Let's just start rattling off words."

"Puke, barf, retch, spew—"

"Upchuck—" Grandpa Zachary added.

"Heave, hurl—"

"Be sick—"

"Purge, maybe. I don't know. I'm sure there are thousands, but that's all I can come up with."

"Then you're in luck," said Grandpa Zachary. "None of those will make good nicknames. What are they going to call you, Barfing Marcus? Actually, that one has a nice ring to it. Don't say it out loud in front of anybody. What I'm saying—poorly—is that stage fright is a normal part of the performance process. It never completely goes away, but it gets better, I promise. And do you want to know the most important thing?"

Marcus nodded. "Sure."

"When you get up on stage and have a good performance, none of your previous bad performances matter. Not at all. You could've regurgitated in front of your class every day for a full week, and it won't take away that amazing feeling of when you do a show and know the audience loves you."

"I'm not doing magic shows though. This was a book report."

"Right. But you get my point, don't you?"

Marcus shrugged. "Not really."

"I'm better at stage patter than advice. But don't worry about what happened today. One day soon it won't matter."

"I'm not sure I can be a magician if I can't even talk in school."

"Yes, you can. I promise."

⌇⌇

TWO YEARS AGO

"Who is that you were talking to outside?"

"Kimberly."

"Is she your girlfriend?"

"No, she just moved here."

"She's beautiful. You'd better snatch her up quickly before somebody else does."

"Yeah, right."

"Confidence, Marcus! Confidence! You didn't inherit my looks, so you stand a chance!"

⌇⌇

ONE YEAR AGO

"Don't ever scare us like that again," said Marcus's mom as the whole family walked out of the emergency room.

"I assure you I was more frightened than you were," said Grandpa Zachary. "But the doctor said I'm the healthiest eighty-eight-year-old he's ever seen. The pieces and parts don't all work as well as they used to, but I plan to outlive you all. And when I say that, I don't mean that I plan for your lives to be cut short. I mean that I plan to live for a ridiculously long time."

"I'm really glad you're okay, Grandpa," said Marcus.

"You have nothing to worry about. I'm not going anywhere. We still have to run away to the circus someday."

5

MARCUS HAD NEVER been to a funeral. His grandparents on Mom's side were alive and well and living in Seattle, while his grandparents on Dad's side—Grandpa Zachary's son and daughter-in-law—had died before he was born. From what he'd seen in movies and on television, Marcus had expected a room filled with sobbing people, but the viewing felt more like a family reunion.

"Eighty-nine years," said Uncle Greg. "That's a pretty good run. Missed a hundred by eleven years though. That's got to be frustrating."

"Yeah," said Marcus, wishing Uncle Greg would go talk to one of the many other available people in the funeral home.

"If you die when you're seventy, that's still three decades away from the big one-oh-oh. It was never really within your reach. But jeez, on his next birthday he would've been *ninety*, and then he'd only have been ten years away. That would really bug me. When you turn a hundred years old, you can basically say or do anything you want. What are people going to do? Put a hundred-year-old guy in jail for strangling somebody?"

"I think they probably would," said Marcus.

"Really? I'd think they'd just let him go. I mean, how many more people can he possibly strangle at that age?"

"I'm not sure."

"When you're a hundred years old, it's not like you can overpower somebody. You're putting some *effort* into that. If I'm a judge and I've got a hundred-year-old man in my courtroom, my thought is, 'Hey, the person he strangled *had* to deserve it.' And even if they didn't, they should've been able to fend off a hundred-year-old man, right? It's like if you walk into a tar pit. It's tragic, but you should've been paying more attention."

"Are you saying that you hope you live to be a hundred so you can strangle somebody?" Marcus asked.

"Well, no, that's not the only reason. Being able to say whatever you want would be pretty cool too. A hundred-year-old man could blurt out the most offensive thing ever, and we'd all just shrug and say, 'What do you expect? He's a hundred. Times were different back when he was born.' I'm not saying that I would necessarily go around saying horrible things, but it would be nice to have the luxury, don't you think?"

Marcus felt like this conversation could use a new direction. "How's Aunt Catherine doing?"

"Oh, if you want to talk about somebody I'd like to strangle when I turn a hundred… No, no, really, she's fine. We're fine. It's great being around her. Every day. Day in, day out, she's always there. No time apart for us, no sir," Uncle Greg said and sighed. "Don't grow up to be like me, Marcus. Hold on to the sunshine in your life. I'm going to go get a handful of those little hot dog things in the croissants. It's great that this funeral home has snacks. Do you want a few?"

"No, I'm okay. Thanks."

Uncle Greg wandered off. Marcus was happy that he left, but now all he could think about was how much he missed Grandpa Zachary.

Somebody tapped Marcus on the shoulder. He turned around, and he saw it was Kimberly. His mood brightened.

She looked fantastic. He'd only ever seen her in jeans and a T-shirt, but of course, that would not be appropriate funeral attire. She was wearing a light blue dress, a dab of makeup, and her black hair hung down over her shoulders instead of being pinned back.

"Hey, Kimberly! I'm glad you made it!"

"I wouldn't miss this," she said, giving Marcus a hug. "I'm so sorry about Grandpa Zachary. He was always really nice to me, and I know how much he meant to you. Are you doing okay?"

Marcus shrugged. "Yeah, I guess."

"There are a lot of people here."

"Yep. For such a cranky old guy, he had plenty of friends." There were at least thirty people in the funeral home right now, and though it was a sad occasion, there was the occasional burst of laughter, probably from somebody sharing an amusing anecdote about Grandpa Zachary.

Kimberly glanced over at the casket. "Why is it closed casket if he died of a heart attack?"

"Grandpa Zachary always said he wanted a closed casket. He didn't want people gawking at his dead body. I don't blame him."

"Are you sure he didn't plan some sort of trick?"

Marcus laughed. "He would. One last prank after his death."

"We should mess with people," said Kimberly. "He'd want that."

"How?"

"I don't know. Maybe tell them the reason it's a closed casket is that he really died in a bullfight."

"His last words were, 'Don't tell *me* that bullfighting should be left to professionals!'"

Kimberly grinned. "Exactly!"

"Or that his last words were, 'Hey, you want to see my new grenade trick?'"

"Or tell people that he decided to become an escape artist. This is his first attempt. Tell them if he's not out in five minutes, they need to rescue him, or he'll suffocate."

"Yes! We could see if we could fool somebody into opening the casket!"

"I bet we could make it happen," said Kimberly. "Working together, we can accomplish amazing things."

"We should've thought about this before," said Marcus. "We could've set up a spring-operated contraption so that when someone opened the casket, his body popped up."

"We could cause heart attacks left and right."

"Drum up business for the funeral parlor."

"Oh, they'd appreciate that. Maybe we could get a commission. What do you think is fair?"

Marcus paused to consider the question. "Fifteen percent?"

"I was thinking twenty."

"Are they covering the cost of the pop-up mechanism in the casket, or are we?"

"They are."

"Then 15 percent is fair."

Kimberly nodded. "All right. Should he be in zombie makeup, or should he look normal?"

"I'd say normal. We don't want to cause a panic. If people get trampled, it's way more work for the mortician than if they just drop dead."

"Are we horrible people for making jokes like this?" asked Kimberly.

"Nope," said Marcus. "Grandpa Zachary would approve." Marcus fought some tears. "Actually, he'd probably say we're making the trick too complicated. Maybe he should just disappear from the casket. We open the lid to show everybody he's inside. And then we close it, wave a magic wand, open it again, and he's gone."

"I honestly can't believe he didn't plan that himself," said Kimberly. "How would you pull off the trick?"

"Easy," said Marcus. For some reason, he always found it easy to brainstorm magic tricks when Kimberly was there to listen to ideas. "Trapdoor in the casket. I'd distract them with the wand while I stepped on a pedal that released the trapdoor, or you'd pull a lever while all the attention was on me."

"So his dead body would drop on the floor?" Kimberly asked, concerned.

"Well, yeah, but we'd put pillows down there."

"Would the pillows muffle the sound enough?"

"We'd have the audience chant something," said Marcus. "If they chanted his name, it would cover the sound of him hitting the pillows. The trick is perfect. Grandpa Zachary would be bummed that we wasted a perfect opportunity. I'm so disappointed."

"It's heartbreaking."

"Promise me that you won't let me die without arranging a trick where I disappear from my casket?" asked Kimberly.

"I can't promise that. You could get attacked by a rhinoceros on the way home today, and then I'd have broken my vow."

"A rhinoceros?"

"Or a hippopotamus. Or a really ferocious meerkat."

"Actually, if I got attacked by a rhino, that would be impressive enough. A magic trick at my funeral would be overkill. I'd want people to talk about the rhino attack, not my body disappearing."

They both laughed. But then despite the lighthearted conversation, the reality that Grandpa Zachary was truly dead hit him. Marcus suddenly wanted to burst into tears, but he didn't want to do it in front of Kimberly. He didn't want to hug her and start sobbing. It would make things awkward later. "Thanks for coming," Marcus said, trying to keep his voice steady. "I should—"

As he glanced around the room, his sadness transformed into anger. What was Bernard Pinther doing here? How did he have the nerve to show up at Grandpa Zachary's funeral?

Bellowing in rage and charging at him was probably not the appropriate way to handle this situation. Nor was flinging ninja stars at him, which didn't matter anyway. Marcus neither owned ninja stars nor knew how to throw them with accuracy. Plus he wouldn't have brought them to his great-grandfather's funeral in the first place.

Marcus decided that the best approach was to ignore Bernard and hope that he'd walked into the wrong funeral parlor by mistake.

Then he realized that Bernard had seen him, and he was

walking toward him. Now would be a good time for Uncle Greg to show up with an armload of hors d'oeuvres. ("Wooo! Free cheese and crackers! Everybody dig in!") But no, his uncle was nowhere in sight. And Bernard was standing before Marcus, clearing his throat, and Marcus was going to have to respond to whatever he said. The wake was about to get really uncomfortable.

"Hello, Marcus," said Bernard.

Marcus squirmed a bit. "Hi."

"Who's your friend?"

"I'm Kimberly." She extended her hand, and Bernard shook it. Marcus hoped that whatever putrid bacteria lived on his hand didn't make her sick.

"Pleased to meet you, Kimberly. My name is Bernard. Marcus, I'd like to offer my deepest condolences about your great-grandfather. We had our differences, obviously, but there was much about him to admire."

Marcus wasn't sure if he should say, "Thanks," or, "Bite me." He went with saying, "Thanks."

"Circumstances have changed since your great-grandfather and I made our wager, and I want you to know that I have no intention of holding you to it. That should be a huge weight off your shoulders."

Marcus had been so upset over the loss of Grandpa Zachary that he hadn't even thought about the performance. His parents had let him skip school, and he'd told his four clients that he'd mow their lawns that weekend. But Bernard was right. It was a relief to know he wouldn't actually have to go through with rehearsing and performing a stupendous trick.

Yet he could imagine the ghost of his great-grandfather, Zachary the Stupendous, hovering over him. *Don't let him cancel the show! This is for my honor! My hooonnnnnnooooorrrrrr!*

But you're dead, Marcus would say. *I was supposed to do this with your help.*

Yes, I guess you're right, Grandpa Zachary's ghost would say. *I didn't think about that. This whole idea is ridiculous and impossible. Forget I said anything.*

Also, you don't believe in ghosts.

You're right. I don't! How hypocritical of me! And then Grandpa Zachary's ghost would vanish.

"Are you all right?" asked Bernard. "You went very pale for a moment."

Marcus stared at Bernard's face. There was something about him that was…well, *evil* was probably taking it too far. Marcus doubted Bernard spent his evenings cackling with wicked laughter and plotting to rule the world. *Mean* was a better description, though maybe that was an exaggeration too. Bernard didn't seem like the kind of guy who would kick a chipmunk in the face. *Arrogant,* Marcus decided. Bernard was arrogant. He thought he was so much better than Zachary, and he thought he was doing Marcus a great big favor by letting him out of their wager.

He is *doing you a great big favor,* said Marcus's brain. *You can't do this show alone. Grandpa Zachary was your coach. Tell Bernard, "Thank you."*

"No, thank you," said Marcus's mouth.

"I beg your pardon?" asked Bernard.

He's offering you an escape, said Marcus's brain. *Take it, you fool! You won't do Grandpa Zachary's honor any favors if you embarrass yourself in front of everybody.*

A different part of Marcus's brain said, *But Grandpa Zachary wouldn't want me to give up. He believed in me. He'd be disappointed if I didn't try.*

You're not giving up, said another part of his brain, the part that usually only thought about potato chips. *Look, none of this was your idea. You didn't agree to this performance. The expectation was that you'd have Grandpa Zachary's expertise available to you throughout the process of formulating this illusion.*

Mmmm, sour cream and onion.

You did not know that Grandpa Zachary would, in fact, be deceased before the process even officially began. Therefore, you are under no obligation, morally or legally, to subject yourself to the anxiety, long hours of practice, and possible high cost of developing this trick.

I hope we've got salsa in the refrigerator. Chips taste better with salsa.

If you accept Bernard's offer to cancel the wager, you are in no way disrespecting the memory of your great-grandfather. Since there's a high risk of humiliation, you are actually protecting his memory.

Hey, it looks like Uncle Greg is eating chips with ridges. There are a lot of advantages to ridges, especially if there's salsa or dip, but I'm not sure I want to go that route today.

Am I babbling? I feel like I'm babbling. You other parts of the brain will let me know if I'm babbling too much, right?

You're babbling, said the part of his brain that had said Grandpa Zachary would be disappointed if Marcus just gave up.

Sorry, said the part of his brain focused on potato chips. *That's why I try not to think too much.*

"No deal," said Marcus's mouth.

Bernard blinked in surprise. "Really?"

"That's right. We made a bet, and I'm sticking to it."

"Are you sure?"

"I'm sure."

"You're only sixteen. That's pretty young to be developing and performing amazing illusions."

"Fifteen. Thank you for the compliment."

Bernard shrugged. "All right. Whatever you want. You'll be the opening act for whatever theatrical performance I have scheduled for that day. If you're not amazing, I'll encourage the audience to boo you right off the stage."

"I can handle booing," said Marcus.

You can't handle booing, said Marcus's brain.

"I'll be in touch. See you in eight weeks. Sorry again about your loss." Bernard nodded politely at Kimberly and then walked away.

"He seemed nice," said Kimberly.

"He's not," said Marcus. "He's terrible. Disinfect your hand with the strongest soap you can find. Or actually, better yet, dunk it in acid for a couple of seconds. Just enough to sizzle off the top few layers of skin."

"So what was he talking about?"

"I have to create a bewildering illusion unlike anything the world has ever seen that will shock, stun, and astonish the audience at Bernard's theater."

"In two months?"

"A little less, yeah."

"Do you have a trick prepared?"

"No."

"Do you know what you're going to do for your performance?"

"No."

"Do you have any ideas?"

"Not really."

"Have you conquered your stage fright?"

"A little."

"Seriously?"

"Maybe. Well, no."

Kimberly looked at Marcus like he was crazy, which he supposed he was, if you reviewed all of the evidence. "And when that man said he'd let you out of the bet, you didn't accept that offer?"

"Nope."

"Are you sure that was the right decision?"

"Nope."

"Do you think you should chase after him and say that you've changed your mind?"

"You don't think I can do it?" Marcus wasn't offended. It was a legitimate query.

"I didn't say that. I'm gathering information. You answered no to a couple of questions where you probably would have answered yes if this was a good idea, but I'm still reserving judgment."

Marcus sighed. "I just feel like I'll be letting down Grandpa Zachary if I don't go through with this illusion. He wanted me to do it. He thought it was a great opportunity to showcase my talent. And it's not like we bet ten thousand dollars or something."

Kimberly narrowed her eyes. "How much *did* you bet?"

"There's no money involved. Grandpa Zachary's honor is on the line."

"How does that work?"

"I'm not sure," Marcus admitted.

"I mean, are you robbed of all honor if the trick bombs?

Does Grandpa Zachary have his honor taken away from beyond the grave? Does Bernard become more honorable if he wins, even though he's basically just humiliating a teenager in front of a bunch of his paying customers? The parameters seem kind of vague."

"It's not the best bet ever," Marcus admitted.

"So you definitely don't want to chase after him? He might still be in the parking lot."

"I'm going to do this. Worst-case scenario, it crushes my dreams of being a professional magician, and I devote the rest of my life to working in retail."

"Well, if you're committed, I'm more than happy to help you out. If you need me."

"Thanks," said Marcus. "I will. I definitely, definitely will."

6

MARCUS SAT IN the back row of biology class while his teacher, Mr. Fuller, talked about the parts of a cow.

Normally, Marcus was an extremely attentive student. Any other day he'd be paying attention to the lecture with laser focus, writing down the names of cow parts as fast as Mr. Fuller could point to them on the full-color diagram. Today, however, his thoughts were occupied with other matters.

A trick. He needed an amazing magic trick.

Card tricks were his favorite, but the scale was too small for those. He could do a trick that involved giant-sized cards where he had to use a forklift to move them around, except Penn & Teller had already invented and executed that trick. Using even *bigger* cards and even *bigger* forklifts would be cool, but probably not in the spirit of this endeavor.

So for now, card tricks were out.

Mind-reading acts were also difficult to pull off on a large scale. And it wasn't an area of magic that Marcus had practiced much. He knew a trick where somebody had to think of a number, and then he could correctly guess what number they were thinking of (which was always eight), but it involved a series of instructions. He would tell the person, "Now divide it by two. Now add three to it," and so on, and the only possible result was the number eight. Having an entire audience simultaneously think of the number eight did not exactly fit the definition of a bewildering illusion.

Also, if people did the arithmetic wrong in their head, it messed up the trick, which made it look like Marcus had messed up the trick. Marcus didn't want to stand in front of a large audience and accuse them of doing the math wrong.

Maybe he could come up with an astonishing variation on one of the classics. How could he levitate somebody in a brand-new way? How could he improve upon the Chinese linking rings? How could he saw a woman in half even *better* than experienced magicians had done it before?

Would that mean cutting a woman into smaller pieces or sawing in half a whole row of women? *Hmm*, Marcus thought. Maybe six women…in boxes placed side by side. He'd just go down the line and saw, saw, saw until all six of them had been halved. Then the boxes would pop open, and all of the women would sit up, completely unharmed. It would be an impressive illusion and also give him the opportunity to work with six hot assistants.

Nah. It was essentially a trick people had seen a million times before. Multiplying the halved women wasn't innovative enough.

"I'm sure you've all heard that a cow has four stomachs," said Mr. Fuller. "That's not entirely accurate. But a cow *does* have four digestive departments."

What if Marcus sawed one woman in half, but when he opened the two parts of the box the two halves popped up and did a little dance? Her top half would float in the air while her bottom half danced around the stage.

This trick would require Marcus to hire somebody to make a full-body cast of Kimberly—that is, if she was willing to be his assistant on stage and let him saw her in half. It would have to be realistic enough that when her torso danced, the audience wouldn't say, "Hey, that ain't the real lady!" (Although if she wore a veil, that could help hide imperfections in the fake Kimberly's face.)

Marcus figured he'd have to hang the torso on wires, and he'd need somebody hiding up in the rafters and manipulating the wires to maneuver it through the air. The legs could also be on wires or perhaps on rods that matched the color of the stage, somebody behind the curtain could control them like a puppet.

This was starting to sound very complicated. Marcus

wasn't sure this was a "can be completed in just under two months while going to school and mowing lawns" illusion. There would need to be an elaborate set of wires controlled skillfully enough that Kimberly looked like she was floating instead of just flopping around in midair. When his school put on a performance of *Peter Pan*, they had the kid playing Peter fly all over the stage in a harness, but the audience was willing to suspend their disbelief to watch a stage play. For a magic trick, the illusion had to be flawless.

Perhaps more importantly, there was no "How'd he do that?" element to the trick. People might be impressed by the technical skill with which it was performed, but they'd still know he'd used wires, rods, and a fake Kimberly.

Mr. Fuller continued on, "The largest chamber in the cow's stomach is called the rumen. It holds food that's been partially digested. How much food? How about up to fifty gallons' worth? You've all heard of a cow chewing its cud, of course, and that cud comes from the rumen."

The cud inspired Marcus. Was there another variation he could do on that trick? Maybe one where he pumped fifty gallons of fake blood out of the box as he sawed someone in half. The fake blood would wash over the stage and cascade out into the audience. Nobody would be fooled by the illusion, but it would be really difficult for Bernard to clean up.

Nope.

Chainsaws! Could Marcus learn to juggle chainsaws in two

months? Maybe he could do a trick in which he juggled the chainsaws and then tossed them onto the box, and then they would saw his assistant in half. Or thirds. Or quarters.

He could juggle oranges reasonably well, but he'd never tried to juggle anything that might dismember him.

If he juggled chainsaws with fake blades and then figured out how to toss them so they landed exactly in the right spot (attached to wires maybe?) and *then* the chainsaws cut through the box (but not for real) without him even holding them, it would be a pretty big twist on a classic illusion. *He'd* be impressed.

Something to keep in mind. Marcus made a note in the margin of his notebook.

"Now the reticulum by contrast can only hold about five gallons of liquid. You'll find lots of cud in there, but it's also where you'll find things the cow shouldn't have eaten like, for example, a rock. If a cow eats a rock and later you slice that cow in half, the rock will most likely be sitting right there in the good ol' reticulum."

What about a vanishing act? Marcus loved vanishing acts. He could make coins, cards, marbles, tiny porcelain frogs, and other small objects disappear with no problem, but he'd never made something disappear that would impress the people in the cheap seats.

One of the most famous magic tricks of all time was when Harry Houdini made an elephant disappear in 1918.

Several other magicians had done variations on the trick since then. What could Marcus make vanish that would have the same impact?

A cow?

No. It would be fun to say that he got his inspiration from biology class, but a cow wouldn't be as impressive as an elephant. And he'd basically just be doing the same trick as Houdini.

A giraffe?

That would be interesting. Could you borrow a giraffe from a zoo? Probably not, but it would certainly be cool to have a giraffe on loan. And yet again, it wasn't a shocking new twist on the theme, just a different animal.

A hundred cats?

He'd get a lot of YouTube hits from that video, for sure. But he didn't want to be responsible for the potential disaster that might arise from having a hundred cats go berserk on the stage. It stopped being cute when members of the audience ran shrieking in agony from the claw marks across their faces.

He'd keep the cat idea in mind though. He wrote, "*Berserk cats,*" in his notebook.

A shark?

Sharks were awesome. Marcus would love to see a magician make a shark disappear. Who wouldn't? Everybody would pay to see that. There wasn't a human being alive on this planet who wouldn't want to see a shark vanish live onstage.

"Wanna see a magician?" "Eh, I dunno. Magicians are kinda lame. What does this one do?" "He makes a shark disappear." "*Whaaaaaat? Take my money! Take my money, you fool!*"

This could be great. His heart began to race with excitement. There were only two problems:

1. Marcus had no idea how to acquire a shark.

2. Marcus had no idea how to make one disappear.

If he was being honest with himself, these were fairly significant roadblocks. But if he successfully pulled it off, his grandpa would have more honor than he could handle. He'd have honor flowing through him like cud through a cow's intestines.

Hmmm. That was a weird and gross concept. Why would that have popped into his mind?

"Marcus?"

Marcus looked up at Mr. Fuller. "Huh?"

"Which chamber sends digested food through the intestines?"

This was not information that Marcus immediately had at the forefront of his mind. He quickly glanced at the diagram Mr. Fuller had been using to guide the class on their tour of the wonderful world of cow innards.

"Omasum?" Marcus could feel the sweat beading on his forehead, but he didn't want to wipe it away and reveal to the other students just how nervous he was.

"No. That chamber is used as a filter."

"Oh, of course. My mistake. Abomasum."

"Correct." Mr. Fuller paused as if he were about to tell Marcus to pay closer attention, but he didn't, robbing Marcus of the opportunity to play the *I just had a death in the family, you monster!* card.

Mr. Fuller resumed the lecture, and Marcus resumed daydreaming about making sharks disappear.

What if he used a real tank with real water, but the shark itself could be computer-generated somehow? Or he could use video footage of a real shark. The only challenge would be the fact that successfully fooling an audience into thinking a real shark had just disappeared would require state-of-the-art technology unlike anything that currently existed. If he could get a hold of several million dollars in development funds and if Bernard could extend his deadline by a few years, Marcus would be all set.

What about a mechanical shark?

Nah. A mechanical shark that could believably pass for a real one would land him back in "several million dollars in development funds" territory. Or maybe just a few hundred thousand. Marcus actually had no idea how much it would cost to create a cutting-edge mechanical shark, but it was more than his lawn-mowing proceeds could provide. And he'd still have to figure out how to make it disappear.

What about a guy in a shark suit? It *seemed* like the stupidest idea ever, but was it really?

Marcus thought about it for a moment.

Yes, it was the stupidest idea ever.

The only way he could successfully convey the illusion was to actually have a real, live shark on the stage. Which *should* mean, if Marcus wasn't completely insane, he'd have to abandon the idea altogether.

For the time being, however, Marcus wasn't willing to rule out his insanity.

He didn't know how he'd get a shark or how much it would cost or if it was even legal or how he'd make sure that nobody got eaten by it, but for now he wouldn't worry about the details. It wasn't as if he was going to use a great white. Surely, he could figure out how to get a hammerhead or something.

Step one? He'd need a huge tank—not merely a huge tank but a huge *gimmicked* tank. This was just supposed to be a five-minute magic trick before a play, so it was entirely possible that Bernard would object to a tank big enough to accommodate a shark being constructed on his stage, especially since it wouldn't exactly be easy to remove. Whatever. Too bad for Bernard. He should've thought of that before agreeing to the bet.

There were two ways Marcus could create this illusion. In the first method, he would show the audience that it was, in fact, a real shark by throwing some fish into the tank. The shark would devour the fish, and the people sitting in the front row would suddenly become very nervous. Dramatic music would play, perhaps the *Jaws* theme, and he'd get the crowd to chant something like, "Shark! Shark! Shark!" as he threw a curtain over the tank. A trapdoor under the tank would open, leading to a hidden compartment in the tank, and the shark, lured by meat, would swim down there, "disappearing" just as Marcus pulled off the curtain for his dramatic reveal.

Or in the second method, he could just use mirrors.

Mirrors were probably a better idea than trapdoors and hidden compartments. He'd have to design the tank so that the people sitting on the sides of the audience wouldn't say, "Hey, that shark clearly just swam behind a mirror!" but it could be done.

This wasn't an illusion that would befuddle experts for decades or even hours to come, but it was a *shark disappearing live on stage.*

Marcus started to think that making a hundred cats disappear would be a lot easier.

Maybe this was a completely ridiculous idea. Maybe there was no way he could possibly accomplish it. Maybe by next period he'd laugh at how foolish he'd been. But right there right then, as he listened to Mr. Fuller talk about cow stomachs, Marcus Millian III, in honor of his great-grandfather, decided to make a shark vanish!

7

AS HE SAT alone in the lunchroom and ate a bologna sandwich like he did every day, Marcus sketched out what his
shark tank would look like. Based on some quick, probably
wildly inaccurate Internet research on his cell phone, a tank
for a hammerhead shark would need to be twenty feet long
and six feet wide at the bare minimum, but probably more
like twelve feet wide since the shark would need to swim into
a hidden section.

That was one big honking tank.

If he were going to keep the shark as a pet (an idea that was
unspeakably awesome but not feasible), he'd need a filter and
a bunch of other equipment to make it a proper aquarium.
Since this was going to be a quick magic trick, in theory all
he needed was the glass tank and the mirror.

He wondered if people were allowed to rent hammerhead

sharks to minors? His parents would probably have to sign off on it. He assumed they would raise an eyebrow or two over the whole idea. He hadn't really told them about Grandpa Zachary's bet. He figured it could wait until later in the grieving process. Their response would probably be a long, confused stare followed by them massaging their temples as if a very strong headache was coming on. And he was sure all that would be followed by a warning. They'd remind him that he was supposed to be saving for college and tell him that he would not be paying for this ludicrous magic trick out of that fund.

Marcus desperately wanted to talk to somebody about the shark trick idea. This was an instance when it would be nice to have more than one friend. Sadly, Kimberly was on a different lunch schedule, so he never had anybody to eat with. This might have been a blessing. She was far from friendless, so while he liked to think that she'd dine with him every day at noon, he might have just sat at his own table, gazing at Kimberly and her female friends from afar.

(But not in a creepy way. Just glancing at them occasionally, not staring or anything. Marcus Millian III was no stalker.)

On the other side of the lunchroom, some kids laughed, which caught Marcus's attention. It was an unpleasant kind of laugh. Not a jolly "Ha-ha-ha, I've just watched a classic silent comedy film that featured a hilarious sight gag!" but a mean-spirited "Ha-ha-ha, that guy fell with his lunch tray, and his food spilled all over. And he's probably too poor to buy another lunch, so he's going to go hungry today. And oh, he broke his leg. Look at the bone sticking out. Ha-ha-ha!"

Marcus hadn't heard a crash or the applause that always followed an act of klutziness, so nobody had dropped a tray. Instead a group of three kids were flicking bits of food at another kid who sat by himself at the next table. The food-flickers were seniors, and so they should have been above this sophomoric behavior. One couldn't except a lowly freshman like Marcus to have matured beyond "Woo! Look at me! I'm a-flingin' my spaghetti!" (Marcus never threw spaghetti at school or home, and if he did, he would not narrate his action in that manner.)

Aside from knowing that they were seniors, Marcus only knew one of the kids personally. His name was Ken, and he was a jerk. This didn't mean the other two kids were jerks. (Marcus preferred to bestow jerk status on a case-by-case basis and not use it as a broad generalization based on some-body's acquaintances.) But based on the ongoing evidence a few tables away, they were all indeed jerks.

The guys were flicking bits of food, which appeared to be grapes but may have been meat loaf, at Peter Chumkin. He was a freshman who'd moved from…Las Vegas? Louisville? Nome? Marcus couldn't remember. All he knew was that Peter was the new kid and that he apparently wasn't a very good student.

Peter was not somebody Marcus would flick food at. He was a giant. Not in an athletic "bulging muscles" sort of way, but there was a height and bulk to him that Marcus personally would not want to taunt. Peter was bigger than all three of those seniors. No way would they act that way if they didn't have the numbers advantage.

As food stuck to his hair, a brown mop that was unevenly cut in the front and covered part of his eyes, Peter went with the classic and completely ineffective technique of ignoring his tormentors. He didn't react. He was definitely aware that bits of food were hitting his body, but he simply sat there, looking kind of sad that it was happening.

Marcus wanted to grab Ken and his buddies by the tongues, drag them into the food preparation area, and dunk them into a vat of coleslaw. But it wouldn't be fair to the students in the later lunch period who'd have to eat the coleslaw. And of course, he'd get beaten up.

The trio of jerks continued their snickering and flicking. Marcus didn't expect Peter to resort to violence by bonking their heads together, but why not at least give them a stern glare? Let them know he was unhappy with their entertainment choices.

It wasn't Marcus's job to defend a big, strong guy against bullies, getting himself flattened into a hamburger patty in the process, so he returned to his sketch.

There were a *lot* of details to work out with his illusion, but as far as he could tell, pulling it off would be really, really, really difficult instead of impossible.

The bullies, growing bolder, flung a much larger chunk of meat loaf (or very old ham) at Peter's head. It struck him in the ear and bounced onto the table. Peter's eyes narrowed, but he didn't turn back to look at them.

Marcus forced himself to focus on his sketch. Peter didn't need his help. After all, he could only distract the bullies for thirty-five to thirty-eight seconds while they pounded him into the floor, after which they would return to throwing food.

The biggest challenge with the tank was that if you saw the sides, it would give away how the trick was done. If he painted them, the audience would say, "Hey, why are the sides of that tank painted? *What is he hiding?*" Marcus would have to come up with a design that looked decorative instead of sneaky. It would also help if he knew the layout of the stage. And the theater seating. And various other factors that he hadn't considered yet.

Still, this was going to be fantastic.

Unless he couldn't get a shark.

But he'd get a shark. He had faith in his ability to get a shark.

He couldn't get a shark. Nobody got sharks.

That's what would make the trick so impressive. Even if the audience wasn't fooled by the illusion, people would say, "Whoa, where'd that kid get the shark?"

He was going to humiliate himself trying to rent a shark.

This was going to work.

This wasn't going to work.

He was headed for glory.

He was headed for disgrace. Dump trucks full of disgrace. Marcus would be standing under a waterfall of disgrace. He'd find little flecks of disgrace between his toes for the next twenty years.

He had to think positive.

No, the smart thing would be to think negative. Then he would be guaranteed to exceed his expectations.

The bell rang. This was good because if lunch continued much longer, Peter would be able to run a buffet line past his hair. Marcus decided to try not to think about sharks for the rest of the school day. He still had about seven weeks to go, and it was best to pay attention in class and pass tests and stuff.

~~~~~

Marcus was unsuccessful in his attempt to not think about sharks for the rest of the day.

~~~~~

After the final bell rang, Marcus walked over to his locker. He'd always wanted to do a trick where he opened his locker and a dozen white doves flew out, freaking out everybody in the hallway, but he didn't think the custodial staff would look favorably upon that idea. And he didn't want any doves to get hurt.

He shoved his books into his backpack, closed his doveless locker, and headed for the main exit. As he turned the corner, he noticed Peter at his own locker. He'd cleaned most but not all of the food out of his hair.

Marcus had probably passed Peter every afternoon for the last month, but this was the first time Marcus had actually paid attention. Peter's locker was far messier than anybody should've been able to accomplish in four short weeks, even on purpose. Peter slowly dropped some books into a brown paper bag, moving as if each book weighed several hundred pounds.

He knew it was weird, but Marcus couldn't help but stand there and watch him.

"Watch it, dork," said somebody larger than Marcus, bumping into him.

Peter finished loading his bag, halfheartedly closed his locker, and walked away. Marcus followed him, trying to decide if he should let him know that there was still a pea in his hair.

He could've caught up pretty easily, but he didn't, choosing instead to follow about twenty feet behind Peter. Following a kid he barely knew down the school hallway was not a typical activity for Marcus, but he figured that he was devastated by the loss of Grandpa Zachary and stressed out by the bet with Bernard, so he could justify some abnormal behavior.

They walked out of the school. Peter walked past the parked busses in the same direction that Marcus walked home each day. Good. This didn't officially become creepy until Peter went in a different direction than Marcus's normal path home.

Marcus noticed that Ken and the other two jerks were also walking in that direction, closer to Peter than Marcus was. What was their deal? They wouldn't really be following Peter, would they? That was nuts. Marcus slowed his pace so that he could better monitor the situation.

As they walked away from school and the crowd of kids thinned, it became clear that yeah, the three unpleasant gentlemen were indeed following Peter. Peter walked extremely slowly, with his head hung, so *not* passing him required that Marcus and the others walk at a rate that was almost a parody of slow walking.

Ken and his pet bullies probably weren't following Peter to compliment him on his fine attire. Were they following him all the way home or just off school grounds?

What should Marcus do? Shout a warning? Pretend he'd forgotten something in his locker and hightail it back to the school, assuming that everything would work out just fine for everybody? Find out if he'd somehow acquired martial arts skills without ever knowing about it?

Marcus just continued to follow the boys. He could decide between the brave or the cowardly approach later.

One of the guys whispered something to the other seniors, and they all had a good, menacing chuckle. Marcus could tell just from their body language that they were going to do *something* to Peter.

Peter turned right at the first corner onto Cricken Street. The bullies followed. Marcus followed the bullies. This was a quiet residential street where, in theory, three seniors would have the chance to beat up a freshman and run off before anybody stopped them.

Peter *had* to know he was being followed. They were maybe ten feet behind him, and they made no attempt to be subtle about it. The guys wanted him to know. That was part of their fun. So shouting a warning wouldn't do any good. And Marcus certainly wasn't going to provide any useful assistance in a fight. His role now was essentially that of the helpless onlooker.

Ken, Jerk #1, and Jerk #2 seemed to come to an agreement, and they simultaneously rushed forward, shoving Peter to the ground.

Peter hit the sidewalk, but he'd braced himself for the impact. He probably knew what was coming. He didn't get up or say anything. He just moved from his hands and knees to a sitting position and stared at the concrete.

Marcus was terrified that the boys might start kicking Peter.

Instead Ken took a can of root beer out of his bag, popped it open, and began to pour it on Peter's head while his buddies howled with laughter.

Why didn't Peter *do* something? He was outnumbered, yeah, but why would he let them treat him like this? If he stood up and raised a fist, Ken would probably drop the root beer and run, yipping like a dog.

Ken emptied the entire can over Peter's head and then dropped it on Peter's head. It bounced off and landed next to him. Peter continued to do nothing and say nothing.

This was too much. Marcus couldn't just stand there and watch.

"Hey!" he said in a loud voice. "Knock it off!"

As the three bullies turned to look at him, Marcus suddenly wished that he were a real magician, one with the power to travel ten seconds into the past to undo previous decisions.

8

SINCE MARCUS DID not possess the ability to travel back in time, he had to accept the consequences of his foolish words.

"Hey, Magic Boy," said Ken, "why don't you mind your own business?"

Marcus was a little flattered. He didn't know Ken knew he was into magic.

Peter looked over at Marcus. He made no effort to wipe at the root beer that trickled down his face, but he did seem relieved to have Marcus there.

"C'mon, guys. There's no reason to do this," said Marcus, even though the opportunity to laugh at another person's misfortune was a perfectly good reason for somebody like Ken to be a jerk. "What did he ever do to you?"

"His very existence makes me sad," said Ken.

"You've had your fun. Leave him alone."

"I don't think my fun level is sufficient," said Ken. "What about you, Chris? Is your fun level sufficient?"

"No," said Chris, "my fun level isn't sufficient."

"What about you, Joe? Is your fun level sufficient?"

"No," said Joe, "my fun level isn't sufficient."

"So," said Ken, "I guess our fun level isn't sufficient."

"That's a strange thing to keep repeating," said Marcus. "I mean, I totally understand what you're saying, but the phrasing is weird. It sounds like something you planned to say instead of something that you just said naturally."

"Are you making fun of me?"

"Not a sufficient amount."

Why had Marcus said that? That was not a smart thing to say. It was, in fact, the least smart thing he'd said in recent memory. Why not just borrow some magic markers and draw a great big target on his face?

Maybe Ken wouldn't get the joke. Being a bully was not typically a high-IQ profession. Marcus's comment might have flown right over his head.

Nope, Ken got the joke.

"Ha-ha. I have a sense of humor about myself, and I admire the way you incorporated my own comment into your comeback," is not what Ken said. In fact, he said nothing. His face contorted into a scowl. His hands clenched into fists. Marcus didn't know if Ken was the kind of guy who heard voices in his head, but if he did, they were saying, *Destroy Magic Boy. Destroy Magic Boy.*

Should Marcus apologize, or was it too late?

"I'm sorry," said Marcus.

"It's too late for that," said Ken. "You want some of what he got? Do you?"

"Uhhhh…do you have another can of root beer?" Marcus asked.

Ken walked toward Marcus, flanked by his two goons.

Marcus supposed Peter would understand if he fled. It was a reasonable response to Ken's building anger toward him. And Marcus couldn't make a shark disappear with two broken arms. (Although, technically, doing the illusion with both arms in slings would make it even more legendary. "That kid didn't just make a shark disappear, and he did it with *two broken arms*!" Still, it was an outcome best avoided.)

But Marcus didn't run away.

With all of the recent talk about honor, he couldn't leave a fellow freshman to be harmed. It simply wouldn't be right.

That was the noble part of his decision. From a more practical standpoint, Marcus knew that he wasn't a very fast runner, so they'd catch him and beat him up worse than if he just stood there.

He needed to talk his way out of this.

What compliment could he use to dissuade Ken from using physical violence? He did have beautiful blue eyes. Ken probably wouldn't take that compliment in the spirit in which it was intended though.

As the three guys entered punching range, Marcus blurted out the first thing he could think of: "Wanna see a magic trick?"

"What?" Ken asked.

"A magic trick," said Marcus, taking a deck of cards out of his pocket. "Do you want to see one?"

"Of course I don't want to see one. What's the matter with you?"

"Actually, I wouldn't mind seeing a card trick," said Chris. "I've always enjoyed those."

"Yeah, me too," said Joe. "My uncle used to do those."

"Are you guys serious?" Ken asked, incredulous.

Chris shrugged. "Sure, why not? Everybody likes magic. You don't like magic?"

"No, I don't like magic," said Ken. "That's for little kids."

"What are you talking about?" asked Joe. "That's not true at all. You're thinking, like, birthday party clowns pulling rabbits out of hats. That's not what magic is all about."

"I'll be honest," said Chris. "I'm eighteen, and I'd still watch a birthday party clown pull a rabbit out of a hat. You don't age out of that kind of stuff. If you don't enjoy magic, there's no love in your heart."

"I agree," said Joe. "I totally agree."

"Who are you? Do I even know you guys?" asked Ken.

"I'm not saying that the freshman's trick will be any good," said Chris. "It'll probably suck. But I don't see how you can dismiss the whole field of magic like that," he said, snapping his fingers to illustrate his point.

"Okay, fine," said Ken. "I don't want to see *his* trick. How about that?"

"That's better," said Chris, "but I do." He looked at Marcus. "Make you a deal. Impress us with your trick, and we won't break your face."

"That sounds fair," said Marcus. He missed the days when he could just do a trick for Kimberly and have her say, "Oooh, cool!" Now everything was high stakes.

He did his most impressive shuffle, which made the cards seem to fly from one hand to the other.

"Wow," said Joe. "How'd you learn to do that?"

"My great-grandfather taught me."

"They're not on a string?"

"Nope."

"That's blowing my mind just right there."

Marcus glanced at Peter. Though he could forgive the fellow freshman for taking this opportunity to crawl away unnoticed, Peter sat there, watching. The root beer still dripped from his hair, though it seemed to have washed out the particles of food left over from lunch.

Marcus fanned out the deck. "Pick a card," he said to Ken.

"I'm not picking anything," said Ken.

"Not even your nose?" asked Joe.

Joe and Chris laughed and then high-fived each other.

"Did you really say that?" asked Ken. "What are you, six years old?"

Joe's smile disappeared. "You're right. That should have been beneath me. I'm sorry."

"You even high-fived him over it."

"Yeah, I shouldn't have been proud of it. I lost myself for a moment there," Joe admitted.

"I wasn't impressed by it," said Chris, "I'm just not one to leave a high-five hanging."

"Well, take it back."

Joe and Chris looked unsure of how to proceed. Then they awkwardly placed their hands together in the air and pulled them away.

"Was that a reverse high-five or just a slow motion high-five?" Joe wondered aloud.

"Stop talking and watch the trick," said Ken.

"Oh, *now* you're interested?" said Chris.

"Should I just go home?" asked Marcus.

"Nah." Ken plucked a card from the deck and looked at it. "Do I show you?"

"Nope." Marcus held up the fanned cards so that the three bullies and Peter could see that they were all different suits and numbers. "Put your card back in the deck."

"Where?"

"Anywhere."

Ken put the ace of hearts (which Marcus knew was an ace

of hearts) back in the deck. Marcus did another impressive shuffle and then fanned out the deck again.

"Is *this* your card?"

All of the cards had turned into the ace of hearts.

"Whoa!" said Chris. "How'd you do that?"

Normally, this was the part where Marcus would look a little smug and say that a magician never revealed his secrets, but he didn't think that smugness was the way to go right now. "Lucky guess."

"What else can you do?" asked Joe.

Marcus returned the deck to his pocket except for one card. He let the card fall out of his fingers…but it floated in midair.

"That's freaky!" said Joe. He reached for the card. Marcus grabbed it first so that Joe wouldn't discover the secret.

"All right," said Chris. "You passed the test."

"Hey, that's not for you to decide," said Ken. "He's just faking us out!"

"Well, uh, yeah," said Chris. "You knew it wasn't going to be actual sorcery, right?"

"That's not what I meant."

"What did you mean?"

"Never mind."

Chris didn't let it go. "No, seriously, what did you mean by 'he's just faking us out' if you weren't referring to actual magical abilities? Did you think he was Gandalf? Explain your reasoning, Kenneth."

Joe laughed and reached up for a high-five but then thought better of it and lowered his arm.

"I'll explain my reasoning with my fist in your face!"

"Now see, you gave Joe a hard time about the nose-picking comment, but that's not any better."

"It wasn't immature. The nose thing was immature."

"But it was weak. You have to admit that it was weak."

"Fine. So it was weak. Not every ad-lib can be a winner." Ken pointed to Marcus. "He's making comments about how it sounds like we planned what we were going to say—"

"Which we did, to be fair," Joe said.

"Don't tell him that!"

"Sorry."

"So if I say something unplanned, you can't go grading it like you're Principal Groutberg."

"Principal Groutberg doesn't give grades. You're thinking of teachers."

Marcus was starting to wonder if this would end with the three bullies beating one another up, leaving him and Peter to casually sneak off.

"Both of you just shut up," said Ken, whose face had become an unhealthy looking shade of red. "Hey, Magic Boy, you think this is funny?"

"No," Marcus lied.

Ken raised his fist. "Do another one."

Marcus just stared at him for a moment. Was that a

legitimate request for another magic trick, or was it sarcasm before he threw a punch?

Three seconds later Ken still hadn't punched him, so Marcus decided that he wanted another trick.

Marcus took a different deck of cards out of his pocket. Ken's fist quivered with rage. If he launched that thing, it was going to be a nose-breaker for sure.

"All right," said Marcus. "For my last trick, you need to pay really close attention. Follow the card." He held up the top card in the deck, a nine of clubs. He put it back on top of the deck and then held the deck in his left hand. "There's a story to this one. Once upon a time, a card committed a horrible crime against the other cards, so he needed to hide. He's trying to hide in this very deck. Do you know where he is?"

Ken hesitated. "Yeah."

"Point to him."

Using his other hand, the one that was not currently preparing to punch Marcus, Ken pointed to the top card.

"Are you sure?"

"Yeah. I mean, I'm probably wrong since it's a trick, but that's where the card went before you did whatever you're doing."

"Okay, so very slowly without letting the other cards see, I want you to slide that card out of the deck. Remember, it's very important that the other cards not see it. I'm counting on you."

Ken, looking dubious, began to very slowly slide the card out of the deck.

"Slower," said Marcus.

Ken pulled even slower. Joe and Chris both leaned forward, watching intently.

"A liiiiiiittle bit slower."

"I can't move it any slower."

"Just a bit. You're doing fine. But don't let the other cards see it. That part is crucial."

Ken continued to move the card one molecule at a time.

Then Marcus punched him in the stomach.

Ken doubled over as the cards spilled to the ground.

Marcus was not proud of this. Using magic to distract somebody before you sucker punched him was not part of the magician's code of ethics. (Presumably.) Magic was supposed to delight and entertain, not cause people to roll around on the sidewalk, groaning in pain.

He could imagine Grandpa Zachary gazing down upon him. "That's not why I taught you these tricks," he'd say, shaking his head in disapproval.

"I know," Marcus would say. "But it's hard enough for me to speak in front of an audience without letting Ken knock out a few of my teeth."

"There's no excuse for what you did," Grandpa Zachary might say. "And I'm afraid I must strongly condemn your behavior, and I hope the shame of what you've done keeps you awake at night, and…are your mom and dad around?"

"No."

"I guess I should have known that already since I'm floating right above you. I don't know why I asked that. So okay, here's the deal. Punching people in the stomach is wrong. You know that, right?"

"Yeah."

"Okay, good. And you know that you should always strive to take the nonviolent approach to work out a disagreement, right?"

"Yes, sir."

"Good. And never waver from that…except maybe when you've got three bigger guys planning to beat you up, and you only got involved because you were trying to stop them from hurting another kid. There's no reason for you to get your face pounded for being a Good Samaritan. Their unfair advantage is that there are three of them, and your unfair advantage is your ability to use misdirection before delivering a mighty blow. So to recap, try not to get into fights, and never do this again. But I'm not going to lie. It was pretty clever. I enjoyed it. Please don't tell your parents I said that, even though I'm dead."

"I won't," Marcus would promise. "Are you in heaven?"

"It's a secret. If I told you that, I'd have to kill you too."

"I understand."

"Anyway, I've got to go. But regarding your idea about making a live shark disappear on stage, what I have to say about that is—"

That's when, if his great-grandfather were really floating above Marcus, he would have faded away because it would have been the most inconvenient time. That's how these things worked.

Of course, this imaginary conversation had happened *really* quickly because there was still running to do.

Marcus sped off.

He quickly realized that he was running in the wrong direction. He should've ignored Peter and run toward his own home, but instead he ran after the kid dripping root beer, shouting, "Hurry! Hurry! Run! Run!"

Behind him, Marcus could hear Chris and Joe laughing hysterically. Apparently, they thought it was hilarious that Ken had been punched in the stomach by a skinny freshman. It did not appear that bullies had tight bonds of friendship.

"Hurry! Hurry! Run! Run!" Marcus repeated as he sped past Peter. This street was a dead end, but if he had to, Marcus would cut through somebody's yard and hope the person didn't have a murderous dog.

"I'll get you!" Ken shouted before he had a coughing fit.

"That was a weak threat," said Chris.

"This isn't—*cough, cough*—over, Magic—*cough, cough*—Boy!"

"My house is the brown one on the left!" shouted Peter.

Marcus saw the small brown home all the way at the end

of the block. He picked up his sprinting pace. He figured that he wasn't really abandoning Peter if he was headed to Peter's house.

He reached Peter's front yard and turned back. Peter wasn't quite running, and he wasn't quite walking. It was sort of an "I don't want any more root beer poured on my head by those guys, but I'm not going to exert myself any more than necessary" pace. Peter didn't seem like he was in bad shape. He wasn't breathing heavy or anything. He just didn't seem like running was worth the bother.

"Hurry!" Marcus shouted as if this would help remind Peter that there was danger afoot.

Ken was still on the ground. Again, there was no glory in a sucker punch to the gut, but it felt good to know that there was actually an instance when Marcus was not somebody others should mess with. Chris and Joe stood around, not trying to help Ken up.

Marcus stood in front of Peter's house and waited. His yard definitely needed mowing. Maybe Marcus could pick up a new customer.

Peter needed to hurry. Why wasn't he hurrying? Any moment now Chris and Joe could stop giggling at their fallen comrade and seek vengeance.

Finally, Peter walked into his driveway. "Want to come inside?" he asked.

"Yes! Yes, I do!"

Peter, still refusing to move like somebody in peril, dug around in his pants pocket for a few moments.

"Ken is getting up," Marcus informed him.

Peter continued to fish around in his pocket.

"He looks unhappy," said Marcus.

Peter took out a key. "Here we go," he said. He unlocked the front door and pushed it open. Without waiting for a formal invitation, Marcus went inside, and Peter, still in no particular hurry, followed.

9

PETER'S HOUSE WAS gloomy, dusty, and did not have a refreshing smell. It was like his family used to have a house-keeper, but she had died during the course of her duties, and her body hadn't been discovered yet.

Marcus peeked out the front window.

"Are they coming?" Peter asked.

Marcus wiped the glass with his hand and then peeked again. "Yeah."

"That's disappointing."

"Well, they're jerks, but I don't think they're psycho killers," said Marcus. "It's not like they're going to try to break down the door or anything."

"Glad to hear that." Peter scratched his head. "Hey, would it be rude if I went and took a quick shower? I've got food and soda in my hair."

"No, sure, go ahead."

"Cool."

"Is anyone going to come home while you're in there? I don't want your mom or dad to wonder why there's a strange kid in your living room."

"Nah."

"Okay. See you after the shower."

Peter walked down a hallway. Marcus returned his attention to the front window. Ken, Chris, and Joe stood at the foot of Peter's driveway, staring at the house.

Marcus looked around for something he could use in the unlikely event that this became a siege situation. There were plenty of magazines to choose from if he wanted to inflict paper cuts. There was also something that looked like a dead dog (which would make a lousy weapon) but on second glance turned out to be a discarded jacket.

Marcus didn't think the seniors were really going to try to break in. But if they *did*, he could scare them away with the moose head on the wall.

Ken, Chris, and Joe seemed to be discussing their options. Then they started to walk away. Joe said something that made Chris laugh, and then they high-fived, and then Ken shoved Joe to the ground, and then Chris shoved Ken to the ground, and then Joe got back up and said something else that made Chris laugh, and then Ken got up, and then the three boys walked off together.

Whew.

Marcus turned on a light on an end table, which made the room exactly 7 percent less gloomy. Now he could see that the walls were covered with moose pictures in addition to the moose head. There were moose everywhere. He'd never considered the possibility that he might develop a moose phobia one day, but if he did, Peter's living room was where it would originate.

The living room also had a large brown couch that might be suitable for sitting on if he brushed away the potato chip crumbs, which actually made Marcus hungry.

He considered walking into the kitchen to peek in the refrigerator, but that would be rude. Instead Marcus peeked out the window to see if the bullies had returned with reinforcements. They were nowhere to be seen. Technically, there was no reason for him to stick around now that the danger had passed. He could call out, "Well, I'll see you at school tomorrow!" and leave.

Nah, that would be impolite…and kind of dumb if it turned out that the Ken/Chris/Joe team was still watching the house. He'd hang out a bit longer.

He took out a deck of cards and practiced shuffling.

The shower stopped. A couple of minutes later, Peter walked into the living room.

"Uh, you missed a piece of meat loaf," said Marcus.

"Where?"

"Over your right ear."

Peter swiped his hand over his ear. "Did I get it?"

"No."

"What about now?"

"Still there."

"Back in a second."

"Okay."

Peter padded down the hallway. He returned a moment later.

"I got it. It was a good-sized chunk too. Surprised I missed it."

"Yeah," said Marcus, unable to think of anything else to say.

"You want something to eat? I was going to make myself a sandwich."

"No, thanks. I'm not hungry."

"You sure? We've got plenty of ham."

"I'm sure."

"You wouldn't be making me go without lunch tomorrow or anything."

"I'm sure."

"We've got fresh ketchup."

"I'm sure."

"Suit yourself." Peter walked into the kitchen. Marcus followed him.

The kitchen was brighter than the living room. Peter took a loaf of bread from a cabinet, and a package of ham from the refrigerator. He began to silently assemble his sandwich.

"So…you like moose, huh?" Marcus asked.

"My mom does."

"What does she like about them?" Maybe a disappearing moose trick might be…nah.

"She likes how the word is the same when it's plural. One moose. Two moose. You can't do that with geese."

"Ah."

Peter opened a drawer and took out a few packets of McDonald's ketchup. He tore the first packet open and squirted some onto the top piece of bread.

"Thanks," said Peter.

"For what?"

Peter shrugged. "For not helping them pour soda on me, I guess."

"Oh, sure, don't mention it. Can I ask you a question?"

Peter tore open a second ketchup packet. "Yeah."

"Why didn't you stand up to them? You're gigantic. They're not brave guys. They would've left you alone if you didn't sit there and take it."

Peter stiffened a bit. "I can't discuss that."

"All right. But you don't have to let them treat you like that. You should have been the one saving me."

Peter stopped squirting ketchup. "You didn't *save* me."

"All I'm saying is that you could have shut them up and made them stop pretty easily."

"Okay, but you didn't save me. You didn't swoop in and save the day, all right? That wasn't a rescue."

"Sure, sure, I know what you're saying," said Marcus, suddenly concerned that there was a block of butcher knives within Peter's reach.

"My reason for not fighting back isn't something I can talk about right now," said Peter as he started applying ketchup to his sandwich again. "And I never will, so don't ask."

"I won't."

"But thank you for punching him."

"No problem. I mean, it will be a problem because now I'm on their radar. I didn't even think of that. Great. The rest of the school year is going to be so much fun."

Peter tore open a third packet. "How long have you been into magic?"

"My entire life."

"Did you do a trick with your umbilical cord?"

"No." Marcus mentally filed away *magic trick with umbilical cord* for future reference, even though it was gross, and he'd probably never use it.

"How'd you learn 'em?"

"Books. Videos. Mostly my great-grandfather though. Have you ever heard of Zachary the Stupendous?"

Peter tore open a fourth packet. "No, I haven't. I'm sorry. I might have seen him, but I don't remember names very well."

"He never really achieved the level of success he deserved. But he taught me lots of stuff."

"I'll have to go see him someday."

"He died a few days ago."

"Oh." Peter looked at Marcus for a moment and then looked at the floor. "I guess I won't then."

"He didn't become a star, but he got to do what he loved. That's what I want out of life."

"Me too. Although I don't really love anything."

"Nothing?"

"Not really."

"You seem to love ketchup."

Peter looked at the top piece of bread. "I do enjoy it. Not something I'd devote my life to. I like the taste, but it's not that interesting to me."

"I was joking."

"Oh. I missed that part."

"Anyway," said Marcus, "I think the coast is probably clear, so I'm going to head home."

"Do you make up any of your own tricks?" asked Peter. He picked up the ketchup-laden piece of bread and, moving quickly so that he didn't spill any, flipped it over onto the other piece. He picked up the sandwich and took a bite.

"Oh, yeah, I love doing that," said Marcus, perking up a bit.

"It must be hard. I'd think that most of the possible magic tricks have already been invented."

"It's a challenge, definitely. I'm going to try to make a shark disappear."

"A real shark?"

"Yeah."

"Where do you get one of those?"

"I have no idea."

"I guess you could steal one from an aquarium."

"I'm not going to steal one."

"Do you know any fishermen?"

"No."

"I'm out of ideas then." Peter took another bite of his sandwich.

"I'll figure it out. I've got almost two months."

"Is it for school?"

"Nah," Marcus said, and then he told Peter all about the bet between Grandpa Zachary and Bernard Pinther. "So you see, it wasn't my idea at all, but I went along with it. I assumed Grandpa Zachary would help me out. Then he died. So I'm basically emotionally devastated, *and* I have to figure out how to do this trick. It's going to be a crazy next few weeks."

"How much did you bet?" Peter asked.

"It doesn't matter."

Peter swallowed the last bite of his sandwich. Marcus was glad to see it go. He was no fan of ketchup.

"Anyway," said Marcus. "I should probably get home."

"How are you going to make the shark disappear?"

"I'm not 100 percent sure yet."

"How *might* you make the shark disappear?"

Marcus decided that it couldn't hurt to reveal his secret,

especially since he had no clue if it would actually work or not. "I'd put a mirror in the tank. It would be at a forty-five degree angle. If I set everything up right, it would just reflect the bottom of the tank. But people wouldn't know they were looking at a reflection, and they'd think they were seeing the whole tank."

"Oh," said Peter, clearly not understanding.

"The tank is divided in half diagonally. The audience only sees the front half. If the shark swims behind the divider, the audience can't see it, even though they *think* they're seeing the entire tank."

Peter nodded. "How do you get the shark to swim to the other side?"

"My hope is that an assistant can drop some meat in there, and the shark will swim over to eat it."

"Won't the audience see the assistant?"

"I have to work out how to hide her."

"Sounds complicated."

"It is."

"Do you worry that your assistant could lose a hand?"

"She wouldn't put her hand in the tank."

"I saw a picture of a shark jumping into the air. You don't want to mess with those things when they smell blood."

"Safety is my first priority."

"How does a shark get delivered to you?"

"I don't know. There are a lot of details left for me to figure out. I'm still in the idea stage right now. I may end up going with a hundred cats instead."

"When you get out of the idea stage, let me know," said Peter. "I'm good at building stuff. I've never built a shark tank, but I bet I could do it. I'd make sure it was safe. You know, like if the shark went berserk, it wouldn't crack the glass."

"Really?" asked Marcus. "What kinds of things have you built?"

Peter shrugged. "Chairs. Couple of bookshelves. A robot."

"A robot?"

"Yeah."

"What did it do?"

"It didn't really do much of anything. But it looked like a robot."

"That's cool. Yeah, I might be able to use your help. Thanks. Anyway, like I said, I've got to get going."

"When a magician turns something into a bird, how do they hide the bird without suffocating it?"

"I can't reveal that."

"I've just always wondered."

"Anyway—"

"Sorry," said Peter. "Don't mean to keep you. Can I say one last thing?"

"Sure."

"I know I didn't do anything when those guys were bugging me today, but if they come after you tomorrow and I'm not around, let me know about it. I'll make sure it doesn't happen again. Okay?"

That sounded more sinister than Peter probably intended. "Uh, okay. Good. Thanks," said Marcus. "See you at school tomorrow."

"See you."

Marcus went into the living room and then peeked out the window one last time to make sure Ken, Chris, and Joe weren't lying in wait. He didn't see them, so he bid Peter farewell and went outside.

Well, *that* had been unusual.

But maybe Peter could be a valuable resource.

Wow. Peter, Kimberly, and him. Marcus practically had a team.

10

AFTER HE FINISHED his homework, Marcus did tank
sketches until it was time for dinner. He didn't tell Mom
and Dad about the shark idea, but he *did* tell them about
his afternoon adventure while they ate fettuccini Alfredo
with chicken.

"Should we call the school?" Mom asked. She sounded
extremely concerned.

"Nah, it's fine," Marcus assured her, hoping his decision
wouldn't turn out to be a fatal one. "I can handle the bullies."

"You shouldn't punch people in the stomach," said Mom.

"I know."

"I agree with your mother," said Dad. "But it's better than
you getting punched in the stomach."

"Dale!"

"It's true! If three older kids are bothering my son and one of them gets punched in the stomach, I'm not going to lose any sleep hoping the kid's tummy doesn't hurt."

Mom looked at Marcus. "You shouldn't punch people in the stomach...or anyplace. There's no good place to punch somebody. If you have to punch someone, punch him with your words. But don't insult people. That's not considerate either."

"I'll never do it again," said Marcus.

After they finished eating and Marcus loaded the dishwasher, he asked if it was okay to ride his bicycle over to Grandpa Zachary's old apartment. He wanted to start going through his possessions to put things in the keep and the donate piles.

"I thought we were waiting until this weekend," said Mom.

"Yeah, but I feel like doing it now. Just an hour or so. It'll inspire me."

"That's fine with me," said Mom. "Do you want me to come with you?"

"Nah, I wasn't going to go through the pictures or anything."

"Are you sure? I don't want you to be there alone if you get upset."

"I'll be fine. I mean, I'm not trying to keep you away, but if I get really sad, I'll call you to come over."

"Promise?"

"Yep."

"All right. Don't stay too long."

Grandpa Zachary's apartment was about three miles away. "Come over whenever you want," he'd always told Marcus, "but don't be surprised if my place is filled with ladies!" Marcus rode over there all the time, though it was never filled with ladies.

The apartment complex was not particularly luxurious, but it was clean and safe. Grandpa Zachary had moved from the second to the first floor a couple of years ago when the stairs finally became too difficult for him to manage.

Marcus unlocked the door and stepped inside.

He immediately wanted to cry, but he stopped himself. He was there to surround himself with inspiration, not to be sad. Marcus closed the door so that the neighbors wouldn't hear if he *did* start bawling, and then he walked around the apartment.

Grandpa Zachary's apartment was a shrine to magic. Posters of all the greatest magicians decorated the walls. Shelves were filled with books about magic. ("Every one ever written!" Grandpa Zachary had said proudly, although this was probably an exaggeration.) Framed pictures of Zachary the Stupendous performing amazing illusions were hanging all over the place.

Marcus didn't really want to think about it, but by the end of the month, they'd have to figure out what to keep, what to sell, and what to donate. For now Marcus just wanted to be surrounded by Grandpa Zachary's things, basking in the environment. He sat down on the sofa and took a deep, relaxing breath.

Then he started to cry.

Grandpa Zachary hadn't been like a father to him. Dad filled that role just fine. But Marcus liked to believe there was a *closeness* between Marcus and his great-grandfather that went beyond their shared love of magic. Even when Grandpa Zachary hadn't been in a good mood, which happened quite often, there was nobody Marcus would've rather spent time with. He didn't know anybody else who even knew their great-grandparents, much less had this kind of bond.

Something rustled in the closet.

Marcus sat up straight.

Did Grandpa Zachary own a pet that he'd somehow failed to mention all of these years?

Another noise came from the closet. It sounded like something fell off a hanger.

Then somebody let out a muffled curse.

Marcus stood up. "Who's there?"

The closet door opened. A man stepped out. He was very old, but it wasn't Grandpa Zachary back from the dead. The man wore a black suit, and his hair was disheveled as if he'd used Albert Einstein as his fashion guide. He held a magic wand.

"Well, the falling coat was unfortunate," the man said. "But at least it spared me standing in there all evening listening to you weep. Who are you?"

"Who are *you*?" Marcus demanded. Then he squinted at him. "No, wait. I think I've seen a picture of you before."

The man smiled, revealing two gold teeth and two silver teeth in addition to the white ones. "Have you? Well, I'm honored."

"Are you Sinister Seamus?"

"Yes! One point for you! And you must be Aloysius."

"No."

"I kid. I kid. I assume you're Zachary's great-grandson, Mark."

"Marcus."

"Left off the *-us*. My apologies."

"Why were you in his closet?"

"Because I didn't want you to see me. That should have been obvious, I'd think."

"I'm serious," said Marcus, trying to sound brave, even though he wasn't feeling that way. "Tell me why you're here, or I'll call the police."

Sinister Seamus held up his wand. "Withdraw that threat, or I'll turn you into a frog."

"Say what?"

"I kid again. I kid again," said Seamus with a smile. Then with one quick motion, he slid off the casing of the wand, revealing a long knife blade. His smile disappeared. "But I'm not kidding now."

Marcus took a frightened step backward.

"Don't move," said Seamus. "If you try anything, I'll cut

you to ribbons. And I don't mean the festive, colorful kind. I mean red ribbons. Do you understand me?"

"Yes, sir."

"Good. I don't like to kill people, especially young ones who have so much to look forward to in life. But I've been put in many a situation where I've had no choice. And I know how to hide a body. Yours will never be found, Marcus."

Marcus tried to force himself to relax. "You're joking, right?"

"I already said I wasn't kidding. How quickly you forget." Seamus chuckled. "Actually, that's not entirely true. I'm seventy-seven years old, and you're…twelve? Thirteen?"

"Fifteen."

"You're young and spry. I doubt very much that I could slit your throat before you ran away or subdued me. The wand-knife is really just for show. But this isn't." Seamus reached into the inside pocket of his suit and took out a pistol.

Marcus didn't immediately pass out from terror, so he considered that a win on his part. He'd naturally assumed that being threatened by three bullies would be the most dangerous part of his day, but the world was filled with surprises.

"Obviously, the problem with shooting you is that it will make a loud bang. This will alert the neighbors and make my escape more difficult. So it's in both of our best interests that I don't have to use this pistol. Do you agree?"

"Yes," said Marcus. "Very much so."

"Excellent. Our relationship is off to a harmonious start then. I feel like our time together is going to end without me having to kill you, and that makes me happy."

"Can I leave now?" asked Marcus.

"No. Once you're out of immediate danger, you'll call the police. That doesn't suit me."

"I won't tell anyone."

"Of course you will. Only a complete idiot would walk out of here and not call the police. *I'd* call the police if I were you. No, this is going to be a bit more complicated than that. Why are *you* here?"

"We have to empty out Grandpa Zachary's apartment before his lease expires. I was going to sort through his things."

"How convenient. I was going to do the same thing." Seamus smiled. "Perhaps we should work together."

"Ummmm…okay?"

"Are you staring at my teeth?"

"No, sir."

"You should. They're interesting teeth. Some people like their teeth to be all the same color, but not me. I've got gold, silver, and four different shades of yellow."

No matter how long he stood there, Marcus did not think he'd ever have an appropriate response to that comment, so he said nothing.

"Anyway, there's something here I need," said Seamus. "I'll give you the medium-length version of the story. When

Zachary and I were first starting in the world of magic, we competed in a contest that was judged by the legendary Quincy Q. Warluck. Have you heard of him?"

"Of course. Grandpa Zachary talked about him all the time."

"Did he tell you what the Q stood for?"

"Quincy."

"Right. His name was Quincy Quincy Warluck. Try saying that five times fast." Seamus chuckled, but then his expression darkened. "I *said*, try saying that five times fast."

"Quincy Quincy Warluck. Quincy Quincy Warluck. Quincy Quincy Warluck. Quincy Quincy Warluck. Quincy Quincy Warluck."

"Very good. I don't see why people think that's so hard. Anyway, there were about twenty young magicians in the contest. Some were immensely talented, and some…well, let's just say that a rabbit got its ears set on fire."

"That's horrible," said Marcus.

"Don't worry. The bunny's fine. I mean, *was* fine. That was almost sixty years ago. I'm not here to talk about bunnies. What I'm saying is that the contest came down to three finalists—me, your great-grandpa, and some other guy."

"Who was the other guy?" Marcus asked.

"I don't remember. It doesn't matter. Why do you even care?"

"To be completely honest, I thought if I proved I was listening to your story, you'd be less inclined to shoot me."

"Oh," said Seamus. "That's not bad logic. But don't ask any more questions, or I'll shoot you."

"Yes, sir."

"So I did a spectacular magic trick where I turned a paper clip into progressively larger paper clips. By the end of the trick, oh, you'd never seen such a big paper clip! You could have clipped thousands of pages with it, and they wouldn't have fallen apart. I can promise you that! Guess what trick Zachary did. Go on. Guess."

"Will a guess count as a question?" Marcus asked. He winced, wondering if "Will a guess count as a question?" also counted as a question.

"No."

"Ummmm, he also turned a paper clip into progressively larger paper clips?"

"No, no, nothing like that. If that had happened, I assure you he'd be dead now. I mean, he'd have been dead sooner. You know what I meant. Guess again."

"He did a card trick?"

"No."

"He did a coin trick?"

"No."

"He did a leaf trick?"

"Why would anybody do a leaf trick?"

"I don't know," said Marcus. "It's hard to make good guesses when you're pointing a gun at me."

Seamus lowered the gun. "He did a trick where he pretended to stick his magic wand in one ear and it came out the other. Does that sound impressive to you?"

"A little."

"Does it sound more impressive than the paper clip trick?"

Marcus shook his head. "Definitely not."

"I know, right? Anybody can do a wand through the head. I'll do a wand through the head right now." Seamus held his wand up to his ear but then suddenly remembered that his wand was in fact a knife. He lowered it again. "The demonstration is unnecessary. All I'm saying is that Zachary's trick wasn't as good as mine. But who do you think won? Go on. Guess!"

"Grandpa Zachary?"

"No, it was the third guy."

"Oh."

"In the short version of this story, I would have left that part out. But when the contest was over and the guy rode off on the pony he'd won, Quincy Quincy Warluck walked over to Zachary, and what do you think he told him?"

"That his magic trick sucked compared to yours?"

"Ha! If only! He told him that his trick was the second best! Can you believe that?"

"*Whaaaaaat?*" Marcus said, pretending that he was very, very shocked by this revelation.

"He did!"

113

"That's a bunch of garbage," said Marcus. "You should have gone over there and knocked him out with your biggest paper clip."

Seamus frowned. "Are you just humoring me?"

"Not at all. It was an appalling miscarriage of justice."

"Don't humor me. The only thing I hate worse than being humored is electroshock therapy."

"Sir, I'm just trying not to get shot."

"Back to my story. Warluck the Wiener—that's the name I gave him later—told Zachary that he saw great potential in him and handed him a small white envelope. And then he said—wait, let me see if I can get his voice right." Seamus cleared his throat and then spoke in a high-pitched squeaky voice. "*Within this envelope is the secret to all magic. Read it, keep it forever, and never share it with anyone.*"

"I don't know anything about the envelope," said Marcus. "Grandpa Zachary never mentioned it." Marcus was kind of surprised by this, even though the anecdote ended with a very specific rule that he should not share the story with other people. Of course, it was possible that this was the kind of story that was completely made up by an insane person, such as, oh, let's say the man standing there with a knife and pistol.

"The envelope is somewhere in this apartment," said Seamus. "We're going to tear this place apart until we find it. And if we don't find it, I'm going to tear *you* apart."

11

"THAT WASN'T A very clever threat," Seamus admitted a few seconds later. "Going from the concept of tearing this place apart to the concept of tearing you apart—that wasn't up to my usual standards."

"It's okay," Marcus assured him.

"No, it's not. You may very well die tonight, and you deserve better threats. You deserve threats that make your blood run cold and your hair stand on end."

Marcus ran his hand through his hair. "It is. See? That was the scariest thing I've ever heard."

"You're humoring me again."

"No, I think you're overestimating the number of times people have said they're going to murder me. I'm a fifteen-year-old aspiring magician. My demographic doesn't get a lot of death threats."

"I suppose you're right," said Seamus. "Now if you were an envelope, where would your great-grandfather have hidden you?"

"In a book?"

"Yes! We are going to rip every page out of every book in his apartment until we find it! Well, no, we'll start by flipping through the pages. No need to ruin perfectly good books. But if we flip through the pages and find nothing, don't think I won't rip those books apart to find hidden compartments! And if we rip those books apart and don't find anything, I will—" Then he interrupted himself. "I can't believe I almost did that same threat again."

"I think you're just tired," said Marcus.

"That has to be it," said Seamus. "I had to take a bus halfway across the country to get here, and the lady I sat next to was just yap-yap-yap-yap-yap about her cult. I got maybe three hours of sleep the whole trip, and of course, my dreams are always about an endless black void, so they weren't restful. I should've gone to a motel and come here in the morning."

"Probably."

"I guess I just need to get over the idea of trying to impress you. When you're dead, it won't matter if I said something witty."

If Sinister Seamus really was exhausted, maybe this was a good opportunity for Marcus to make a daring escape attempt. He might be able to knock the pistol and knife out of the old guy's hands.

"Don't even think it," said Seamus.

"Think what?"

"About using my lack of sleep to your advantage. I don't have to be a mind reader to know what's going on in your head."

"I wasn't considering that," Marcus fibbed. "I'm way too cowardly."

"Very well. I'm going to sit down on this comfy-looking couch, and you're going to search the books. If I feel like you're trying something sneaky, I'll shoot. If I feel like you're not searching to the best of your ability, I'll shoot. If I fall asleep and my finger accidentally squeezes the trigger, I'll shoot. There are quite a few scenarios where you'll get shot, so my advice is to search as quickly as possible."

Marcus walked over to the first bookshelf. He decided to start with the top left, a hardcover book titled *Magic for People Who Think That People Who Do Magic Tricks Are Total Losers* by Aaron Aackles. He slid the book off the shelf and opened to the first page, and a small white envelope fell to the floor.

"Did that really just happen?" asked Seamus, rubbing his eyes.

Marcus picked up the envelope. The letters "Q Q W" were written in a very fancy manner on the back.

"Give it to me!" said Seamus, setting down his weapons. "Quickly!"

Marcus handed him the envelope.

Seamus cackled with mad laughter. "Yes! I've awaited this moment for decades! The secret to all magic is finally mine! All I had to do was not die before Zachary Millian!"

Since Seamus was now distracted, Marcus wondered if this was the proper time to make a move. After all, Marcus had a hardcover book he could use to whack Seamus on the head.

No, Seamus had what he'd come for, and hopefully, he'd apologize for the inconvenience and for Marcus's possible permanent emotional scarring and leave.

Seamus opened the envelope and removed a white card.

He smiled.

He opened the card.

He looked at it for a moment.

The smile remained frozen on his face, but his eyes, which had been so merry and twinkling, did not convey the same "I'm happy!" message as his mouth.

The edges of his smile began to falter. Then gravity completely took over, and his smile transformed into a scowl of unspeakable, unfathomable, uncheerful rage.

"Are you *kidding* me?" he bellowed. "Is this some kind of cruel joke? I waited six decades for *this*?"

Seamus held up the secret to all magic. Written in black ink was one word—*Practice*.

"Practice? Practice? I knew that! Everybody knows that! That's no big secret!"

"To be fair," said Marcus, "the secret to all magic really is to practice. It's not like the envelope had bad advice."

"I thought the secret held the key to the universe! I thought this secret was going to change everything for me! Practice? Seriously?" Seamus tore the card into several pieces and flung them to the floor.

"I don't mean any disrespect," said Marcus, "but as much as I love Grandpa Zachary, it's not like he was ever a superstar in the world of magic. Don't you think that if he knew the ultimate secret, he'd be the most famous magician ever?"

"I figured he squandered the secret!" said Seamus. He picked up the knife and the gun, and now Marcus regretted not whacking him in the head with the book when he'd had the opportunity. "This is unreal! I can't even describe how upset I am right now! I need to destroy something!"

"You can destroy the couch," offered Marcus.

Seamus slammed the knife into the couch cushion and then shook his head. "No, this isn't satisfying."

"I think there are some eggs in the refrigerator."

"No."

Marcus thought for a moment. "He's got a ventriloquist's dummy in the bedroom. You could pretend it was a person."

"No, those things creep me out."

"Maybe you just need a nice, brisk walk."

"Never mind. The urge to destroy something has passed."

Seamus sighed. "That long bus ride for nothing. Did I mention that a bug crawled into my ear?"

"Nope, you did not mention that."

"It might still be there. I can kind of feel it squirming around next to my brain, but of course, I feel that even when there's not a bug in my ear."

"Will you be leaving soon?"

"Not quite yet. I need to get *something* out of this trip. Tell me about this wager."

"Oh, um, how did you know about that?"

"Magic."

"Grandpa Zachary and Bernard Pinther made a bet that I couldn't do an amazing trick at his theater."

"And you're confident that you can?"

"Well, no, I'm not the one who made the bet."

"What trick do you have in mind?"

"Making a shark disappear."

"Hmmm," said Seamus. "I can see potential there."

Marcus would've loved to have an experienced magician helping him out, but since Seamus had repeatedly threatened to kill him, Marcus doubted his viability as a good candidate.

"What's at stake?" Seamus asked.

"Honor."

"Zachary had no honor. Bernard has no honor either. They're betting for something nonexistent. The winner of the bet might as well receive a unicorn."

"Yeah, well, like I said, I'm not the one who made the bet."

"Those stakes aren't interesting at all. But perhaps…" Seamus's smile didn't quite return, but the corners of his mouth perked up a bit. "Tell me, Aloysius, do you believe that true evil exists in the world?"

"I, uh, guess I believe that everybody is capable of doing good things and bad things."

"They say that everyone is the hero in their own life story," said Seamus. "I'm not. I'm the villain. I love being evil. Just love it. I am literally the most evil person you will ever encounter. I go by the stage name Sinister Seamus, but that's just to lull you into a false sense of security. When you hear the name Sinister Seamus, you figure, 'Oh, this guy is going to be a little scary, but it's nothing I can't handle.' Wrong. Dead wrong."

Seamus was smiling again. Marcus couldn't deny it. Seamus did indeed seem to love being evil.

"If this were a musical, I'd do a song right now about how evil I am. Sadly, real life is not a musical, and if I launched into the 'I'm So Evil' song, you'd just give me an odd look."

"You could record the song beforehand and just play it at the appropriate time," Marcus suggested. "That would be less awkward."

"That's an interesting idea."

"There are some kids at school who are in a band. They'd probably be happy to help you out."

"I wasn't legitimately disappointed that people in the real world don't break into spontaneous musical numbers, but you're making me think," said Seamus. "If some people had you cornered and they suddenly started playing a song about how evil they were, you'd be frightened, right?"

"Petrified."

"Something to consider. Anyway, where was I?"

"Your evilness."

"Right, right. What I'd like to do is make your bet more interesting. Let's say, for example, that your life depended on winning. That would make the wager more interesting, don't you agree?"

"No," said Marcus. "That would be boring. Totally bland."

"Oh, don't be such a spoilsport. This is going to be fun." Seamus tapped one of his teeth with the knife. "Here's the deal. If your magic trick doesn't meet the minimum level of amazement to win the bet, I will find you and kill you."

"I don't think that will inspire me to greatness."

"I believe it will. Did you know that the cure for measles was invented at gunpoint? It wasn't. I just made that up. But it would've been interesting. What are you staring at?"

"Your silver tooth fell out."

Seamus glanced at the floor. "Oh my, I guess it did. Happens every time I tap it with the knife. I have to remember to stop doing that."

"Do you want me to pick it up for you?"

"Nah. I'll get it on the way out."

"Okay," said Marcus, relieved.

"You're probably thinking that you're not in any real danger because you'll just call the police when you leave this apartment. That would be a very bad idea. That would be worse than the time Benjamin Franklin tried to pierce George Washington's tongue with a wooden nail. Which I just made up. Being evil, I lie a lot."

"You were lying about killing me if I lose the bet too, right?"

"No, Aloysius, that was the truth. Before I distracted myself with fun facts about our founding fathers, I was getting to the part where I explained *why* talking to the police would be such a bad idea. I'm a magician. The police will never catch me. I've killed lots and lots of people and haven't been caught yet. If you try to get me in trouble, I won't just kill *you*. I'll kill your mother, your father, and your sister, and I'll flush your goldfish."

"I won't say anything," Marcus promised.

"You probably felt a bit of relief just now, *Marcus*, because you don't have a sister or a goldfish. And that relief has vanished because you've suddenly realized that I know this. I know many things about you. If I wanted to kill you and the rest of your family, believe me, young man, I could do it."

Marcus felt more than a little queasy. "Don't hurt my mom and dad," he said. "I won't tell anybody."

"That's a most excellent answer indeed. I may seem like a

bumbling fool, but I promise you, a percentage of my foolishness is an act for your benefit. You may feel braver once we're no longer having this conversation, but I cannot stress enough how bad of an idea it would be to defy me. Do I need to carve a reminder onto your arm?"

"No," said Marcus. "You really don't."

"Glad to hear it. So how will you determine if you've won the bet or not?"

"I'm not sure."

"Audience vote? A panel of judges? Applause-o-meter?"

"We haven't worked that out yet," Marcus admitted.

"How can you have a wager without determining the criteria for winning?"

"Like I said, it was all very spur of the moment. I don't even know if Bernard Pinther will let me have a giant shark tank on his stage."

"Sounds like you have a lot of work to do."

"Yes."

"I'll still kill you if you don't win."

"Oh."

"Anyway," said Seamus, reaching down and picking up his tooth, "I suppose it's time for me to depart. Best of luck on the task ahead of you. Good night." He gave a polite wave and left the apartment.

"Well…bummer," said Marcus before he got completely dizzy and fell onto the couch.

12

MARCUS HAD TWO options.

1. *Tell the police that there was an evil magician on the loose who had threatened him and his family if he didn't win a ridiculous bet.*

2. *Not tell anybody.*

To figure out whether to choose option 1 or 2, he had to decide which of the following was more credible:

1. *Sinister Seamus could indeed evade the authorities and then go on the promised murder spree.*

2. *Sinister Seamus would be immediately apprehended by the authorities and spend the rest of his life pouting in prison because Marcus hadn't played along.*

His gut feeling was that option 2 was more likely, but if the correct answer turned out to be number 1, it would be the worst wrong answer he'd ever given on a multiple choice quiz.

What if he just canceled the bet with Bernard?

1. *Seamus would say, "Oh well," and move on with his life.*

2. *Seamus would say, "That's a violation of the rules!" and go slash, slash, slash with his knife-wand thing.*

Again, option 2 seemed more likely.

He couldn't tell anybody what had happened. If he did, he'd be putting those he loved at risk. Marcus had to win the bet. He'd have to make the shark disappear.

Marcus staggered into the kitchen. His throat had gone dry. He opened Grandpa Zachary's refrigerator and peered inside. His options were:

1. *bottled water* or

2. *apple juice.*

He went with number 1. He drank the entire bottle in one gulp (well, seven or eight gulps, but one big swig). Then he had to clutch the counter to keep himself from losing his balance. He'd never been this terrified in his life. Which made complete sense. What other times should he have been more terrified?

Maybe Seamus was just kidding. Maybe he had a really dark sense of humor and thought it was funny to make a kid think that he had to pull off an amazing illusion or die. Maybe he thought it a delightful prank. The options were:

1. *Seamus was joking* or

2. *he wasn't.*

Marcus had to go with his second thought.

He left the apartment and rode his bicycle home. When he walked into the living room, Mom and Dad could tell something was wrong, but they seemed to assume he was upset about Grandpa Zachary and not a random encounter with a gun-and-knife-wielding madman. So Mom gave him a big hug, which was comforting but insufficient to calm his nerves.

That night Marcus had plenty of nightmares.

The next day at school, he tried not to think about sharks and evil magicians and to instead focus on what his teachers were saying. It was a challenge. When Mr. Parker announced a pop quiz in the last ten minutes of history class, Marcus froze. He hadn't heard a single word of the lecture.

"This one will be easy," said Mr. Parker, handing out the papers. "Just making sure you were awake."

Marcus glanced at the first question. It might as well have said, "In what year did Zagglehoggenfritz eclipse the mutton-chopped 245x371.98 45dms7ifg42?" The other four questions were no easier to answer. He wrote, "I don't know the answers to any of these questions, and I humbly apologize," at the bottom of his quiz, hoping he'd at least get a point for humility.

He didn't think he could handle a lunchtime encounter with the trio of bullies if they were looking for him, so he ate his lunch on a bench outside. He hoped that Ken, Chris, and Joe weren't wreaking vengeance upon Peter at this very moment, but there wasn't much he could do if they were. He didn't think they'd fall for another card trick distraction.

He needed to relax. If he really did end up getting killed by Seamus, he didn't want to waste his last seven weeks on earth being stressed out.

Yet, Marcus remained stressed out for the rest of the school day. Fortunately, there were no other pop quizzes, although he was pretty sure he missed some crucial information about the Pythagorean theorem in math class.

When he got to his locker after the final bell rang, Peter was waiting for him.

"Hey," said Peter.

"Hey," said Marcus.

"What's going on?"

"Nothing."

"Didn't see you at lunch."

"No."

"Detention?"

"I ate outside."

"Oh."

"Sorry."

"Are you on your way to detention now?"

"No. Are you?"

Peter shook his head. "Nope. You want to come over?"

"I can't. I've got a lot of work to do on the trick. We should walk together though. Safety in numbers."

"I started on the shark tank," Peter said.

"Seriously?"

Peter gave him a sheepish smile. "Yeah."

"I haven't even finished designing it yet," said Marcus.

"I know. Just gathering materials. Glass and stuff. Thick glass."

"Where'd you get it?"

"Can't talk about that."

"Is it stolen?"

"Can't talk about that."

"I can't do a magic trick with stolen materials."

"I'm no thief."

"Seriously, Peter, if I get arrested, I'll lose the bet."

"Is that a rule?"

"No, but I can't afford to lose the time I'd spend locked away."

Marcus wondered if Sinister Seamus could get to him in jail. Maybe going to prison for being an accessory to glass theft was the way to keep himself alive.

"Trust me," said Peter.

"I barely know you."

Peter looked at the floor. "Yeah, you're right. I was just trying to help."

Marcus closed his locker. "Believe me. I need all the help I can get. Anything legal you can do would be great."

Peter looked up and smiled. "Okay."

As they walked out of the school building, Marcus froze. Somebody was in the parking lot, waiting for him.

"What's wrong?" Peter asked.

Bernard saw Marcus and motioned him over. Marcus didn't really want to talk to him. But then he decided that it would be one of the less dangerous conversations he'd had lately.

"I have to talk to this guy," said Marcus. "If you want to wait for me, that's cool. Otherwise, I'll see you tomorrow."

"I'll wait," said Peter.

Marcus walked across the parking lot to where Bernard stood. He didn't look happy.

"Hi," said Marcus.

Bernard handed him a small poster. "Explain this."

It was a photo of Marcus dressed in a black tuxedo and top hat, waving a magic wand at an immense tank in which a great white shark swam. Big dramatic words proclaimed, *See Marcus the Stupendous Perform His Amazing Vanishing Shark Illusion! Pinther Theater. Friday, January 13. 2:00 p.m. Parental Discretion Advised.*

"Uuuuuuuuhhhhhhhhhhhhhhhh," said Marcus.

"I'm waiting."

"Where did you get this?"

"They're plastered all over my theater. And on every business in a six-block radius. Do you know how many complaints I've had about posters being put up without permission? We never agreed on a date or a time. I understand that you're young and your brain hasn't fully developed, but what made you think this was okay?"

"I didn't do it," said Marcus.

"Then who did? Zachary back from the dead?" Bernard frowned. "I'm sorry. That was inappropriate. If you want to make a tasteless remark about one of my deceased relatives, I'll allow it."

"No, that's okay."

"I understand that your great-grandfather and I let our emotions get in the way of rational thinking, but I still have a theater to run. You can't go putting up posters without consulting me. I assume your trick will be terrible, so I have to keep audience expectations low!"

"I said I didn't make the posters." It was a pretty cool poster though. The image was clearly done in Photoshop, but whoever designed it had added filters to make it look like a poster from a hundred years ago.

"Then who did?" Bernard demanded.

In the bottom right corner were two tiny letters—S. S.

"I don't know," said Marcus.

"Are you saying the posters just magically appeared? Is that what happened? Are you such an astoundingly talented magician that your publicity materials appear by themselves? Wow, what a trick! David Copperfield might as well quit now because there's a new master in town!"

"I don't know what to tell you," Marcus said. "It wasn't me."

Bernard studied him. "Why have you gone pale?"

"Excuse me?"

"Your face was normal-colored when you walked over here, and now you're pale. You look frightened. What's wrong?"

"Nothing."

"Is it me? Am I too intimidating? I could scale back my assertiveness if that's the issue."

"No, I'm fine."

"Why do you keep looking at that one specific corner of the poster?" Bernard asked.

"No reason."

Bernard took the poster from him and studied it. "S. S." He suddenly went pale too. "Sinister Seamus?"

Marcus avoided his gaze. "I don't know who you're talking about."

Bernard lowered his voice. "Did Sinister Seamus contact you? Old guy. Two silver teeth and two gold ones. Pure evil."

"I—"

"I won't breathe a word to him, I swear. But I have to know how much danger you're in. Does Sinister Seamus know about the bet?"

"Yes," Marcus whispered.

"Oh no," said Bernard. "That's bad, Marcus. It's very, very bad. Worse than bad. Do you know how many people he's killed? Guess."

"Fourteen?"

Bernard let out a snort. "If only! Oh, what a happy,

sunshiny day it would be if Sinister Seamus'd killed a mere fourteen people. Guess again."

"A thousand?"

"Now you're just being silly. Obviously, he didn't kill a thousand people. What did he say to you?"

"He said he wanted to raise the stakes and that if I didn't win the bet, he'd kill me."

Bernard closed his eyes and rubbed his forehead. "Doomed," he said. "You're doomed. Sinister Seamus may seem a little dopey, but I assure you, he's a criminal genius. There's nothing dopey about him. Do you know why I keep a severed finger in my desk drawer?"

"I didn't know you *had* a severed finger."

"Well, I do. Do you want to know why?"

"I kind of don't."

"I keep it there because Sinister Seamus sent it to me…as a reminder."

"A reminder of what?"

"A reminder that he could send a finger to me anytime he wanted! That's how evil he is! And if he's paying attention to our wager, then you absolutely have to win. Have you finalized how your disappearing shark trick is going to work?"

"No. Not at all."

"Well, you'd better do it before January 14."

"Can't we cheat a bit?" asked Marcus. "What if we set it up so that only one member of the audience has to enjoy the trick for me to win? I'll have a friend come and pretend to be shocked and amazed."

"Sinister Seamus will never allow that. It has to be a legitimately successful illusion, or terrible things will happen. Don't go thinking that your demise will be quick and painless. Have you ever seen *Return of the Jedi*?"

"Of course."

"Do you remember the Sarlaac Pit, where it takes a thousand years to be digested?"

"Yes," said Marcus, feeling sick.

"Of course, you'd die of old age before the thousand years was up, so it's not a perfect comparison, but you get what I'm saying. You *have* to make that shark disappear. You have no choice."

"I don't even know if I can get a shark!"

"All I can say is that you're better off draping some raw meat over your shoulders and jumping into the ocean than you are facing Sinister Seamus. Don't even try to change your identity. It won't work. Edgar Wooverton, formerly Clifford Simmons, knows that all too well."

"Gosh darn it," said Marcus, approximately.

"Sorry I made your day worse," said Bernard. "Don't worry about the posters."

Bernard got in his car as Marcus walked back to Peter.

"That looked upsetting," said Peter.

"It was. There literally wasn't a single sentence of that conversation that I enjoyed."

"Whoa, that's awesome!" said Peter, noticing the poster in Marcus's hand. "I had no idea your magic show was going to be that cool! I'm so glad I get to be part of it!"

"I hope we deliver."

"We will. And if not, no big deal. It'll be the first of many shows."

They walked silently until they reached Peter's street, where Ken, Chris, and Joe were waiting for them.

13

"YOU'RE IN FOR it now," said Ken. He punched his open palm with his fist, obviously trying to convey the message that Marcus's face could be punched in the same manner.

"Nah," said Marcus. "I'm not interested."

"What do you mean you're not interested?"

"Just what I said. I've got a lot of problems right now, and you're low on the list. Honestly, getting beaten up by you guys would be way more enjoyable than dealing with what's happening in my life."

Ken looked confused. "You understand that I'm threatening to cause you extreme pain, right?"

"Of course. It's not about a lack of awareness on my part. It's about ranking. Don't get me wrong, you're awful, but I've got worse things going on."

"But…we're going to beat you up. It would be better if you were terrified."

Ken looked to Chris and Joe for help. They both just shrugged.

"What could be worse than us beating you up?" Ken asked.

"I can't talk about it."

"I don't believe you."

Marcus shrugged. "That's not my problem. Look, if you want to beat me up, go right ahead, but I'll be thinking about something else the whole time."

Ken lowered his arms. "Maybe we'll do it some other day then."

"That's probably for the best."

"C'mon, let's go," said Ken, walking away. Chris and Joe followed him.

"That went better than I thought," said Peter. "I figured at least one of us would end up unconscious."

"Would you have fought back?"

"Nah."

"That still doesn't make sense to me. As a scrawny guy, I understand my own hesitation but not yours."

"Just can't do it," said Peter.

"Why not?"

"Can't talk about it."

"All right. Well, I'm going to stand here for about thirty seconds so that I don't catch up to them while I'm walking the rest of the way home."

"Do you want me to wait with you?"

"You might as well."

"I will then."

"Thanks."

"Are you timing it?"

"No. It doesn't need to be exactly thirty seconds."

"Okay."

"Don't start building anything yet."

"I haven't."

"I'm sure there are some federal guidelines about tanks holding sharks in front of an audience. I'll research all of that and get back to you."

"I'll get more glass in the meantime."

"You know these will need to be huge pieces of glass, right? Not smaller pieces glued together."

"We'll work it out."

"I feel like maybe you don't understand the concept."

"It'll be fine."

"I don't want you to put in the effort if it's material we can't use."

"Don't worry about me."

"Magic is an exact science."

"Got it."

"I'll see you tomorrow then?"

"You sure will."

Marcus began to walk away.

"Hey, Marcus?"

Marcus stopped. "Yeah?"

"Can I ask you a favor?"

"Sure."

"It's kinda pathetic."

"That's okay."

"I mean, I don't even want to ask."

"Does it involve popping zits on your back?"

"Nah."

"Then it'll be okay. What's the favor?"

Peter hesitated. "My mom worries about me a lot. I told her you came over yesterday, and that made her happy. But I sort of think she thinks I made it up."

"She thinks you made *me* up?"

"Yeah, I make up stuff sometimes. This one time she called me from work, and I told her that Dad came back because I thought it would make her feel better for a little while. But she knew it wasn't true."

Marcus frowned. "So your dad left you guys?"

Peter nodded. "Yeah, about four years ago. He didn't have a girlfriend or anything. He just didn't like having a wife and a kid, I guess. I hid the note he left because I thought it would be better if he went missing on accident instead of on purpose, but my mom found it and got really mad."

"You never see him?" Marcus couldn't imagine never seeing Dad.

"Nah. Don't even know where he is."

"I'm sorry."

"Not your fault. Anyway, my mom doesn't get home from work until around nine. And I know this is stupid, but I was wondering if you could come over and, I don't know, lend me a book or something."

"Lend you a book?"

"I just want my mom to know that you're real. She works hard and deserves a better son, and I thought it would make her happy if she thought I'd made a friend at school who'd lend me a book."

"Sure, yeah, I can do that. What kind of books do you like?"

"I don't know. A lot of times the words just don't line up right. Do you have a beginner's guide to magic?"

"I've got several of them. I'll bring one."

"Thank you. I'm probably the most pitiful friend you've ever had, if you even think of me as a friend, which there's no reason why you should. Don't tell anybody I asked you this favor, okay? Make fun of me in your mind, but please don't make fun of me to other people."

"It's totally okay," said Marcus. "I won't even make fun of you in my mind."

"I'm not good at ending conversations, so I'm just going to go home." Peter turned and walked away.

I guess I've got another friend, thought Marcus as he walked home. Honestly, though he wouldn't say this to Peter, friend was maybe too strong of a word just yet. They didn't have much in common, and Peter wasn't all that easy to talk to. But

Marcus wasn't willing to rule out the possibility that they'd become friends in the future, which seemed a lot better for his social life than just hanging out with Kimberly sometimes.

As soon as he stepped onto his front porch, Marcus's cell phone vibrated. It was a text from Kimberly: Practice canceled. Want to talk magic? He wasn't sure if she meant soccer, cello, or *Oliver Twist*. (It was hard to keep track of her schedule.) But he definitely wanted to talk magic.

Absolutely!!! he texted back.

That's a lot of exclamation points.

Should I tone it down?

No, I'll let you know if it gets out of hand.

Thank you!!! I appreciate that!!!!!!!!!

Okay to come over now?

Yes!!!???!!!???@#$%&!

On my way.

Except in this particular instance, where Marcus was purposely overusing and misusing punctuation marks for comedic effect, one of the things he really liked about Kimberly was that they both used correct grammar and spelling in their text messages.

After dumping his backpack in his room, he went to the refrigerator to get Kimberly and himself something to drink—a can of delicious, sugary, maximum-calorie soda for him and a can of nasty, sugar-free, zero-calorie diet soda for her. He didn't know how she could drink this stuff.

Then he went upstairs to brush his teeth. Though Marcus had excellent dental hygiene, his typical regimen involved brushing and flossing in the morning and in the evening. He wasn't prone to midday brushing unless he knew Kimberly was on her way. He didn't think there was anything wrong with this.

A few minutes later, the doorbell rang. Since Halloween was over, the doorbell no longer let out a piercing shriek.

He opened the door. For a split second, he worried that Seamus would be standing there. Or to a lesser extent of worry, Ken, Chris, and Joe. But no, it was indeed Kimberly.

"Hi," she said as she walked inside and tossed her backpack on his couch. "How're you holding up?"

"I'm fine."

"You sure? You look a little haunted. And it's like you've aged. You could pass for seventeen or eighteen now."

"Stressful week." Marcus handed Kimberly her soda. "Wanna go up to my room?"

"Okay, yeah."

Marcus's mom and dad loved Kimberly, and they wouldn't care if she was in his room when they weren't home because they knew nothing would happen. Marcus was perfectly aware that nothing would happen, but he did sort of wish that his parents would forbid her from being in his room, to float the possibility that their trust that nothing would happen might be misplaced.

Kimberly scooted out Marcus's desk chair and plopped down on it. She popped open her soda and took a big drink. "What amazing ideas have you come up with?"

Marcus suddenly realized that he hadn't told her about his plans yet. He'd had too much on his mind, what with all the peril. "The magical vanishing shark."

"Interesting," said Kimberly. "So your trick is to destroy their natural habitat and drive them to extinction?"

"Nope. Not enough room on the stage for an entire ecosystem."

Kimberly laughed. "That's why you're the magician and I'm the magician's assistant. Although everybody knows the assistant does all of the real work."

Very often, that was true. When a magician slid a whole bunch of swords into a box, it was the assistant inside the box, twisting herself into the right position and guiding the blades to create the illusion that a dozen swords had stabbed through the box without poking her.

"Don't worry," said Marcus. "I won't make you get in the tank with the shark."

"What's it going to be? A puppet?"

"No, a real shark."

Kimberly set her drink on a coaster on his desk. "What?"

"I'm going to try to get a real shark for the trick."

"Have you discussed this with others?"

"A couple of people, yeah."

"And did they try to dissuade you?"

"Not passionately."

Kimberly paused to consider this. "Maybe I need more information. You mean a tiny shark, right? Something that's technically a shark but is the size of a trout?"

"No," said Marcus. "I mean a full-size, nightmare-inducing shark. A shark that would make lifeguards close a beach."

"Interesting."

"You think it's a bad idea?"

"It's definitely not the concept I anticipated when I heard about the bet."

"Do you think I'm not going to be able to pull it off?"

"There are some ideas that aren't about whether you *can* do something. They're about whether you *should*. My concerns aren't like that. This is all about whether you can. How are you going to get a shark, Marcus?"

"It's on my to-do list."

"I hope it's near the top."

"I wanted to be sure I could make a shark disappear before I looked into how to get one."

"I feel like it should be the other way around," said Kimberly. "When you told these other people, what was their reaction?"

"I guess there was some confusion. A little disbelief. Maybe a smidgen of sympathy for my mental state."

"What did your parents say?"

"It's possible that they don't know yet."

"Possible?"

"Probable."

"Probable?"

"I mean, I haven't told them, but they could be spying on me. If they've got me under twenty-four-hour surveillance, I'd assume they've heard about it."

Kimberly sighed. "Do I have to be the voice of reason?"

"It's too late for reason." Marcus opened up his backpack, took out the poster, and handed it to her. "I'm committed."

"Ooooo-*kay*," said Kimberly. "So it looks like you're making a shark vanish."

"Yep."

"Then let's work this out."

14

"ARE YOU GOING to rent a tank or build one?" Kimberly asked.

"Probably build one," said Marcus, pulling another chair over to his desk and sitting down next to her. "Or buy one and do some major customizing. Do you know Peter Chumkin?"

"I don't think so."

"You'd know him if you saw him. New kid. Started about a month ago. Gigantic."

"Stares at the floor all the time?"

"Yeah."

Kimberly nodded. "I see him in the hallway. Does he own a shark tank?"

"No, but he says he can help me make one."

"He's kind of weird, don't you think? Don't get me wrong.

That's not a bad thing. But can he really help you build a shark tank?"

"He's not the most normal person I've ever met," Marcus admitted. "And I haven't seen anything he's built. But I can't do this all by myself, and letting him help can't hurt. I mean, it can hurt if the tank shatters and I get hit with broken glass. Or if one side of the tank comes loose while I'm crouched down next to it. Actually, there are lots of ways you can get hurt when you're dealing with large pieces of glass…and a shark. So yes, letting him help can hurt."

"Glad we sorted that out."

"I don't completely know Peter's role yet. All I know is that he was grateful when I saved him from the *three* bullies, and he offered to help."

"Hold up," said Kimberly. "I feel like I missed a story somewhere."

"It's not important."

"Yes, it is. You emphasized the word *three*."

"Did I?"

"Yes. Just a little."

"It wasn't on purpose."

"I'm sure it was subconscious. But you can't just throw out a comment about saving somebody from three big, bad bullies and then not fill me in on the rest of the details. Who were they?"

"Do you know Ken?"

"The senior? That jerk?"

"That's the one. It was him and two of his friends. They were picking on Peter, and—"

"Peter could squish them like blueberries!" Kimberly interjected.

"I know. But he didn't. So I told them to stop and—"

"How did you say it?"

"I just asked them to knock it off."

"Right, but were you polite? Did you shout it? Did you go all action hero on them? I need details here."

"I know you won't believe me, but I said it in a loud, stern voice."

"Let me hear it."

"*Hey!*" Marcus said in a slightly louder and sterner voice than he'd actually used, but it wasn't *too* much of an exaggeration of the truth. "*Knock it off!*"

"Wow." Kimberly looked impressed.

"I got caught up in the moment. If I'd taken the time to consider what I was doing, I probably wouldn't have told them to knock it off."

"And so they scattered at the power of your words?"

"Yeah."

"Really?"

"No."

"What happened?"

"I tried to reason with them."

"With Ken? No way did that work."

"No. Basically, Ken held up his fist—"

"What was Peter doing while this was happening?"

"You're making it difficult to tell the story."

"You're leaving out crucial details."

"He was on the ground."

"Sitting? On his back? Unconscious? I don't hear a lot of stories about bullies being defeated, so I don't want you to rush through your moment of glory. Brag about it."

"It's not really that big of a deal," said Marcus.

"I'll be the judge of that."

Marcus backtracked to the beginning of the story in the cafeteria, where he'd first noticed bullies throwing pieces of meat loaf at Peter. As he told his tale of bravery and hero-ism, he wondered if Kimberly would be impressed by the part where he gut-punched Ken when he wasn't expecting it or if she'd think it was a low-down, dirty trick. Maybe he should recalibrate the story. Just a bit.

"So Ken was staring at the card. I had his complete undivided attention. Then I said, 'Is *this* your card?' and punched him in the face."

"You really did that?"

"Yep."

"You're not making it up?"

"If I were making it up, I would have said that I said something more clever. 'Is this your card?' doesn't actually make much sense. I wish I'd said something different."

"Wow."

"It was a crazy day."

"You saved Peter. Well done."

"Don't use the word saved around him though. He's sensitive about that."

"Why?"

"I'm not sure. I guess he doesn't like the idea of being rescued by somebody with twigs for arms."

"That's reasonable. You can't expect him to start referring to you as 'My hero!'"

"Nope."

"Back to the shark tank. Have you figured out what you need?"

Marcus opened up his notebook and showed her his most recent sketch. "The mirror reflects the bottom of the tank, and the audience thinks they're seeing the whole thing. My original thought was that we'd have a detailed backdrop on the stage and that a rectangular piece of it would be duplicated on the bottom of the tank. That way, people would think they were looking right through the tank at the full backdrop. But it would have to be an absolutely perfect match, and we'd have people watching from too many different angles for it to work. So I ditched that idea. It's just going to be a neutral background. Maybe light blue or something."

"Can't go wrong with light blue."

"I hate the idea that we can't have clear sides to the tank, but if we do, people will see the mirror. I don't think there's any way around it. It could explain why the world doesn't see a lot of tricks involving fish disappearing from aquariums."

"We'll make a goofy cartoon drawing of a shark and put one on each side," said Kimberly. "The audience will think it's funny and part of the entertainment, not realizing that we're hiding something."

"That works."

"How do you get the shark to go on the other side of the mirror?"

"Feed it."

"And who will be doing that?"

Marcus did not immediately answer.

"Uh-uh," said Kimberly. "Feeding a shark falls outside of the scope of our friendship. If you want a one-armed girlfriend, be my guest, but it won't be me."

"What?"

"Huh?"

"What did you say?"

"I said that if you wanted a one-armed friend, you should be my guest, but that it wouldn't be me."

"Oh, I misheard part of it."

"You should listen more carefully."

"In the future, I will."

"Good."

Kimberly was blushing. Not a scorched-face type of blush, but she was definitely aware that she'd inadvertently added the word *girl* to the word *friend*.

Marcus wondered if he should just come right out and say, *You know exactly what you said. And you know you meant it. Let's stop pretending and accept the way we feel about each other.*

No, he should definitely not just come right out and say that.

Based on Kimberly's look of discomfort, his best move was to proceed as if she hadn't made any accidental compound words in recent sentences.

"You wouldn't actually put your hands into the tank," Marcus clarified.

"Nope."

"You'd drop in the food from a safe distance above the water."

"Nope."

"I can find somebody else to do the feeding part," said Marcus.

"Maybe Peter will do it. He owes you. How exactly do you get food into a shark tank that an entire audience is staring at?"

"Well, that's another one of the thousands of challenges. They won't actually be able to see *through* the tank, they will just think they are. So somebody could hide behind it, and they would never know."

"But we'd see their hand when they drop in the shark chow."

"The water wouldn't go all the way to the top," Marcus

explained, pointing to the sketch. He had a wavy line to represent the water. "There'll be a hole in the back of the tank just above the waterline where somebody can drop the food."

"Gotcha. How do you know for sure that the shark will go for the food?"

"That's what sharks do, right? I read somewhere that they can smell blood in the water from miles away. If we throw bloody meat into a tank and the shark leaves it alone, then we've been lied to about sharks all these years."

"Won't the audience see the blood in the water?"

"The food will be in the water on the other side of the mirror. The worst that can happen is that it gets a little cloudy."

"The worst that can happen is that the shark breaks through the mirror in its thirst for blood," Kimberly pointed out.

"Oh, it could be a lot worse than that," said Marcus. "Safety precautions will come after I figure out all the logistics of the illusion."

"Next logistical question: How does the shark get to the other side of the mirror? If you leave a gap for it to swim around, people will see it. And if I'm envisioning this right, which I may not be, when the shark swims to the other side of the mirror, it will just kind of—how can I describe this?— wipe away? Like in a movie when they wipe from one scene to the next. Do you know what I'm saying?"

Marcus nodded. "You're right. The mirror has to go all the

way across the tank, or it's totally obvious how we did the trick. But it's got a—"

"Wait. I see it," said Kimberly, tapping the sketch. "There's a hinge in the mirror. I thought that said *bingo*."

"What would bingo mean in a shark tank?"

"No idea. I was waiting for you to explain it. Maybe you were planning to distract the audience with a game of bingo while you moved the shark from one side of the mirror to the other."

"Nope, it's a hinge. Whoever feeds the shark will tug a wire that drops the hinge. Once the shark is where it needs to be, they'll tug the wire again to pull the hinge back up. The wire will be looped around a small hook, but I haven't figured out how to hide that yet."

"This doesn't sound easy," said Kimberly.

"No, it's pretty much going to be the opposite."

"You could do a card trick," she suggested.

"Not an option. And I don't want this to be easy. It's not supposed to be easy. I'm not gonna lie. I wouldn't mind if it were a little *easier*, but I don't want it to be easy."

"If the trick doesn't go as planned, at least you'll know you did your best."

"Right," said Marcus. "Although I'd really like it to go as planned."

"Of course. But if it doesn't, you can say that you put in a lot of effort and didn't take the easy route. That's something

Grandpa Zachary would be proud of even if the shark doesn't disappear."

"Yes, I agree. However, I'd very much like for the shark to disappear."

"I'm sure it will. All I'm doing is saying that if it *doesn't*, you shouldn't feel bad. What you're trying to do is incredible. It's the first of a long line of amazing performances you're going to give as a professional magician. So even though you should work hard to make your stage debut the best it can be, don't fall into despair if it doesn't turn out perfectly. That's all I'm saying."

"And I appreciate it," said Marcus. "That being said—"

"The shark trick might not work," said Kimberly. "We're going to do everything we can to make sure it's a success, and I'm confident that it will be. But if it's *not* awesome and amazing, I want us to be able to refer back to this conversation when I said that it would still be okay, so you don't think I'm just making it up later."

"As long as we try our hardest." *Something to engrave on my tombstone*, Marcus thought.

"I knew you'd see it my way," said Kimberly.

And then she kissed him.

15

FOR A MOMENT Marcus and Kimberly sat there, noses touching, staring at each other. Then Kimberly pulled away.

"I'm sorry," she said.

"No apology has ever been less necessary," said Marcus, surprised that he was able to speak any words at all, much less a word with four syllables.

"I don't know what came over me."

Marcus hoped it was his intense animal magnetism, but then he said, "It's fine. Actually, it was great."

"No, it's not," said Kimberly, pushing back the chair and standing up. "I messed up."

"Why? Do you have a boyfriend you didn't tell me about?" he asked, hoping he was kidding.

"Of course not."

"Then what's wrong?"

"Ninety-nine percent of the time, I don't see you that way. Okay, ninety-eight. There's nothing wrong with you, nothing at all. It's just not how I feel. If I did, we'd have gotten together two years ago."

"That makes sense," said Marcus slowly. He felt weirdly ashamed, even though he'd done nothing wrong—that is, except not being the kind of person to whom Kimberly was attracted.

This was terrible, disappointing, and embarrassing. However, in the grand scheme of things, Grandpa Zachary had died, and Sinister Seamus had threatened to kill him, so it was only the third worst thing to happen to Marcus this month. (The encounter with the bullies was better than this.)

It's not so bad, said one part of Marcus's brain. *She thinks of kissing you 2 percent of the time! And look at the bright side. At least you got to kiss her.*

Shut up, said all of the other parts of his brain.

"Can we just pretend that didn't happen?" asked Kimberly. "Make it disappear like a shark?"

"I guess we—"

"No, no, no, you don't kiss somebody and then tell them to get amnesia. We're not going to pretend it didn't happen. We just won't dwell on it. Sound okay?"

"Sure."

"You can mention that it happened. In that moment you were irresistible. Does that sound like I'm leading you on?

I'm not trying to. I really don't know what to do here. Help me out, Marcus."

"We'll joke about it once a week."

"Yes, that's a plan. That's a fine plan. Excellent one. That's how we'll deal with this. I should go home now."

"Don't go," said Marcus. "We won't start the jokes until next week. I still need to talk through the shark trick."

"I think we've pretty much covered it, don't you agree?"

"How are we going to hide the shark going through the hole in the mirror?"

"You were going to throw a curtain over the tank. At least that's what it shows in the drawing."

"I just think it's something we should discuss out loud. Is it too much of a cheat to use a curtain? Penn & Teller wouldn't do a trick with a curtain."

"How else would you do it?"

"I don't know. More mirrors?"

"I'm not a reflection expert, but that feels like too many mirrors."

"You're right. It's an abundance of mirrors."

"A plethora of mirrors."

"A ton of mirrors."

"A bunch of mirrors."

Marcus had to think for a moment. "A lot of mirrors."

Kimberly frowned. "See, even our repartee is forced now. I messed everything up between us."

"You didn't mess anything up," Marcus insisted. "I can totally ignore it. I'll act like I got hit in the head with a brick."

"Before I kissed you, we would have stopped at 'a ton of mirrors.' We would have naturally sensed when to quit. Now we fumble onward. I knocked our instincts out of whack."

"We'll get it back in whack." Marcus redirected the conversation. "So you're right. I'm not a fan of curtains in magic tricks, but there's probably no way around it. I mean, we could shut off all the lights for a few seconds, but that's kind of the same concept. Plus, if somebody takes a cell phone picture during those few seconds, we'll look stupid."

"There's no shame in a curtain."

"None."

They were both silent for a moment.

"See, we should have been able to riff on that," said Kimberly.

"No, I think you're being overly sensitive. If this conversation happened five minutes ago, you wouldn't be worried that we weren't riffing on the curtain comment. We'd just let it go and move on. Now you're analyzing everything we say."

"You're right. I've created the condition where I feel as if I need to compare the way we're talking now to the way we were talking before."

"Let's just talk and not worry about it," said Marcus.

"I can't. It's in my brain now."

"Let's get back to the curtain. We'd need to do everything with split-second precision. I throw the curtain over the tank, and somebody immediately releases the hinge while dropping the shark bait. Once the shark goes through, they need to get the hinge back up as soon as possible so I can tug the curtain off again."

"It all has to happen really fast," said Kimberly. "How can you be sure the shark will go straight for the bait?"

"Maybe we starve it for a while? No, we can't be cruel to an animal, not even a killing machine. I don't know. Honestly, I guess we need to test it and desperately hope for the best."

"And if it doesn't work at least—"

"*Desperately* hope for the best."

"I should go now," said Kimberly. "I'm sorry I wrecked our easygoing vibe."

Marcus wanted to assure her again that he could ignore what'd happened, but every time he did that, a sliver of his self-esteem was shaved off like a slice from a block of cheese. He was in danger of becoming an object of pity and didn't want a relationship that was based on her thinking, *Aw, poor li'l fellow.*

"Whatever you need," he said.

"No, I should stay. No, I should go. No, I should—" Kimberly stood up. "It would be easier if you told me to get out of your room."

"Not gonna do that."

"Here's what I'm going to do. I'm going to leave, but I'm going to get you a live shark for your trick. I don't know how, but I'm taking on that responsibility right here right now. I'm not going to reach my hand over the tank to feed it, but I'll get you a shark. How does that sound?"

"You don't have to do that."

"Not legally, but I think I should."

"It might be impossible."

"I'll take that risk."

"It might be really expensive."

"I'm not actually volunteering to pay for a shark. But I'll set you up with the means to get the shark."

"Ah, okay," said Marcus. "I appreciate that."

"I'll keep you posted."

"Thank you."

"Thank you for the Diet Coke. That was very generous."

"Anytime."

"I'll let myself out."

"Okay."

Kimberly walked out of his room. Marcus just sat there for a while. Until recently, the weirdest month of his life was when he was seven and got bitten by two different parakeets. Now he felt like he was in this strange alternate reality where everybody had gone insane, including him.

He couldn't worry about the kiss with Kimberly, even if it was perhaps the greatest thing that had ever happened. As with the bullies, he had more important concerns than this amazing life-changing moment. It would be challenging to win Kimberly's heart if an evil magician skewered him and roasted him over a campfire.

He looked at his sketches again.

This trick wasn't going to work.

He was deluding himself. Even with the help of his friends, he didn't have the resources to get a shark or build a fancy mirrored tank. He might as well do a trick where he leapt off a skyscraper and drifted to the ground using a plastic baggie as a parachute.

He should cancel the bet and call the police.

Seamus couldn't possibly be *that* dangerous and clever. The guy wasn't a vampire. He couldn't transform into a bat and fly in through an open window. The very idea that Marcus was frightened for his life was kind of silly.

Or was it?

Bernard didn't seem to be the kind of person to overreact. If he thought that Marcus should be trembling in fear, it was probably accurate.

Marcus wanted to pound his head against his desk, but he decided that acquiring a head injury would not be conducive to solving his problems. Best to keep his brain in top working order.

He decided to compromise. He took the pillow off his bed, placed it on his desk, and then hit his head against it a few times. Then a few more times. Then another dozen. He didn't feel any better. Not even when he stopped.

Maybe he should take up stress-eating. That had to accomplish something.

What about a good old-fashioned primal scream?

He probably shouldn't scare the neighbors.

He settled for letting out a muffled primal scream into the pillow, which didn't do much to ease his anxiety level.

Marcus should've fled the fund-raiser when Grandpa Zachary had asked him to do a trick in front of everybody. That's when all of this started. If only he'd completely chickened out, his life would be normal now.

Or if he'd done a *better* trick, Bernard might have said, "Hey, kid, nice work," and none of this would've happened either.

It was no good to dwell on the past, except for the brief distraction it gave him from the present. Maybe he'd wait until he knew with 100 percent certainty that he wouldn't be able to pull off the illusion and then call the police. No reason to do it before that.

"Why is your pillow on your desk?" asked Mom, startling Marcus so badly that for an instant he thought the solution to all of his problems might come if his heart exploded. He grabbed for the edge of his desk as his chair tilted back. The chair legs slid forward, and he crashed to the floor anyway, bonking his head.

"Marcus!" Mom cried, crouching down beside him. "Are you okay?"

"Yeah, I'm fine."

"I'm sorry. I didn't mean to sneak up on you. I assumed that you heard me come home."

"I was distracted," he said. Mom helped him to his feet.

"Well, that's understandable," she said, though she only knew maybe a third of the story. "You know you can always talk to us, right?"

"I know. Nothing's new," he said, lying to his mother as if telling an audience that there was nothing up his sleeve while packing eight bunnies in there.

"Did you want to take a nap?" Mom asked.

"No. Why?"

"You have a pillow on your desk."

"Just working out a trick."

"It's not a smothering trick, is it?"

"Everybody involved in the trick has full access to oxygen."

"It's going to be tough, but you'll get through this, Marcus. Dad and I are always here for you." Mom squeezed his shoulder. "What's this?" she asked, picking up the poster.

Marcus glanced at the poster as if he were seeing it for the first time. "That's the trick I'm doing at Pinther Theater for Grandpa's angry bet."

"You're making a shark disappear?"

"Yes. Hey, is it okay if I go over to a friend's house after dinner?"

"Kimberly's?"

"No, his name's Peter. I'm going to drop off a book."

"Oh, sure. How's Kimberly doing?"

"She's confused about some things right now." Marcus supposed that technically Kimberly wasn't confused about anything. She was simply regretting her momentary lapse into fiery passion. Marcus felt no need to share this with his mother.

"I'm surprised you two are just friends," she said. "I've seen the way you look at her."

"How do I look at her? Is it creepy? Please tell me it's not creepy."

Mom smiled. "Nothing like that. I just think you two make a cute couple. I've seen the way she looks at you too. You should ask her to a movie."

"We've gone to movies."

"Ask her formally."

"You mean print up an invitation? Deliver it in a horse-drawn carriage?"

"You don't have to be sarcastic. You know what I mean. Pay her way in. Bring her flowers. Buy her Raisinets."

"And what if she sees me as nothing but *friend, friend, friend, friend, friend, friend* on an endless loop?"

"What's the risk?"

"If she says no, it ruins everything, and suddenly, the only women I ever talk to are my teachers and you."

"Trust your mother."

"No offense, Mom, but I'm putting 'trust your mother' in

the category with the tooth fairy and getting eaten by the refrigerator monster."

"I never said anything about a refrigerator monster."

"I guess that was Dad."

"That's horrible! I'll have to talk to him about it."

"I was six, Mom."

"Well, I knew it wasn't last month. But he shouldn't be saying things like that."

"It kept me from sneaking pudding cups at night," Marcus offered.

"Well, if we have another kid, he won't be telling him or her about the refrigerator monster."

"You're having another kid?" asked Marcus, slightly horrified. He really *was* living in an alternate reality.

"No."

"You're thinking about it?"

"No."

"Are you sure?"

"It was purely hypothetical," his mother reassured him.

"You promise?"

"You don't want a little brother or sister?"

"I did ten years ago. That ship has sailed."

"It's not something you have to worry about."

"I *wasn't* worried until you started throwing out all this new kid talk!"

"You're the one who brought up the refrigerator monster."

"Yeah, but that doesn't mean you need to have a baby. My heart and mind are fragile. You've got to think about what might set me off."

Then Mom gave him a hug. "I apologize for messing with your fragile mind."

"I'm going to do my homework now."

"Okay. I'll let you know when dinner's ready."

Mom left his room. She had given Marcus many, many pieces of good advice over his lifetime, everything from "Treat people with respect" to "Don't stick that pinwheel up your nose." But man, she sure had botched her advice about Kimberly.

16

AFTER DINNER, MARCUS picked out his most basic book, *Magic for the Bumbling Incompetent.* It had sections on how not to poke yourself with scissors when doing a rope-cutting trick and where to get change for a dollar bill in case you needed coins.

He walked over to Peter's house and knocked on the front door. Nobody answered. He started to ring the doorbell, but then he noticed that it had a thin layer of translucent yellow sludge on it, so he settled for knocking again.

Finally, the door opened a little, and Peter stuck his head out. "Oh, hey, Marcus."

"I brought your book."

"Thanks. That was really cool of you."

"Did you want me to—" Marcus didn't think it was a good idea to say "prove my existence to your mother" in case his mother was standing right there.

"Ummmm. Yeah, yeah, that's a good idea." Peter opened the door all the way. An extremely thin woman lay on the couch, mouth open, snoring loudly. "Hey, Mom? Mom?" Peter turned back to Marcus, looking fidgety and sheepish. "I don't think she's going to wake up right now."

"That's okay."

"I'm going to put a blanket on her and then come out. Give me a second."

"Sure."

Peter closed the door. He opened the door again a second later. "Forgot the book."

Marcus gave him the book. Peter glanced at the cover, ducked back inside, and closed the door after him.

Peter took long enough that Marcus started to wonder if he should just leave, but eventually, Peter opened the door again and stepped outside. "Sorry about that," he said. "She had a rough day."

"I understand."

"Wanna go for a drive?" Peter suggested.

"We don't want to get our learner's permits taken away."

"I've got my real license. I'm sixteen."

"I thought you were a freshman."

"I am a freshman."

"Oh, okay. Sure, where do you want to drive?"

"Wherever."

"It's a school night. We can't be gone that long."

"We won't be."

Peter unlocked the car, and Marcus got into the passenger seat after he brushed some candy bar wrappers onto the floor. The car smelled a bit like gasoline, though for his own comfort, Marcus decided to pretend that it was because of a gasoline-scented air freshener hanging from the rearview mirror.

Peter started the engine, backed out of the driveway, and drove off.

"Nice car," said Marcus.

"Thanks. If my mom gets a new car, she's going to give me this one." He stopped at a stop sign, carefully looked both ways, and then turned right.

"When's she getting a new one?"

"Probably not until this one's completely dead. So it's not really much of a deal for me."

"That sucks."

"Yeah. I'm saving up for one though."

"Are you close?"

"Nah."

"That sucks."

"Yeah." Peter sighed. "I don't really feel like talking that much. Can we just listen to music?"

"Sure."

"What've you got?"

Marcus took out his phone. "I'll be honest. I haven't got much of anything but Weird Al."

"Weird Al's cool."

"Okay."

Marcus plugged his phone into the stereo and set his Weird Al music library on shuffle. The polka medley seemed to make Peter more cheerful, and after a couple of minutes, Marcus thought he might be able to temporarily forget about his own problems too.

After about twenty minutes, Marcus asked, "Should we head back?"

"Not yet."

They listened to two more songs before Marcus said, "Now I feel like we should head back."

"We're not there yet."

"I thought you said we were just driving."

"We are…mostly."

"Are you kidnapping me?"

Peter laughed. Fortunately, it was a "ha-ha, that was funny" laugh and not a "he-he, now you understand the true nature of this little drive" laugh.

"No," he said, "you're not being kidnapped."

"Then if I still have free will, I'm requesting that we go back home."

Peter scratched his chin. "I trust you, Marcus. You've been a good friend so far. I'm ready to talk about why I didn't fight back."

"Okay," said Marcus, intrigued. "Let's hear it."

"Not here. Five more minutes."

Marcus decided not to protest and added "riding with Peter" to the list of his recent poor life choices.

He wasn't familiar with where they were driving. It wasn't necessarily the kind of neighborhood he would choose to travel through when it was dark. In fact, when Peter finally stopped the car in front of a long-abandoned convenience store with boarded up windows and broken glass all over the ground, it was pretty much the last place Marcus would have said, "Hey, I know. Let's park here!"

Peter shut off the engine.

"So, uh, this is our destination, huh?" Marcus asked.

Peter nodded.

"I can't think of any positive reason we might be here... unless you have bars of gold hidden inside. Is that why we're here? Even then deadly people could be after the gold, so that wouldn't be a positive reason either."

"We'll be okay."

"I'm sure we will because even the criminals don't seem to want to be here when the sun goes down. Seriously, Peter, my parents would have a stroke if they knew we were here. Just tell me what we're doing so I can stop thinking that you're offering me up as a sacrifice."

Peter cracked his knuckles but didn't say anything.

Marcus sighed. "I wish I'd have brought a mugger's wallet."

"What's a mugger's wallet?" Peter asked.

"It's a second wallet that you carry around in case you get mugged. Like a decoy. I don't have any money in my real wallet, so they're going to demand flesh."

"I won't let anybody mug you," Peter promised.

"Are you going to jump in front of a bullet?"

"If I have to."

Peter seemed 100 percent serious when he said that, which made Marcus even more nervous.

"Fine," said Marcus. "I'm going to stop having a panic attack and let you say what you brought me here to say."

"Do you promise not to laugh at me? I can't have you laughing at me."

"I won't laugh."

"Most people would laugh at me."

"I will try not to be like most people."

"Promise me."

"Why didn't you ask for the promises before we left? Now I'm invested. If you've got restrictions on my behavior, set them before I ride with you for half an hour into a post-apocalyptic wasteland."

"You're right," said Peter. "That was unfair. How about this? You can laugh, but I need you to promise that you won't make fun of me either to my face or to anybody else."

"I promise I won't make fun of you."

Peter stared into Marcus's eyes for a very long time. Finally, he blinked, apparently satisfied. "I couldn't fight back against those bullies because I needed to protect my secret identity."

Marcus was silent for even longer than Peter had stared into his eyes. "What?"

"If I defeated them, they'd know what I was capable of, and I can't allow that."

Marcus was puzzled. "What?"

Peter unfastened his seat belt, turned around, and leaned into the backseat of the car. He picked up a brown paper sack, set it on his lap, and unrolled the top. He took out a rubber witch mask and put it over his head.

"When I wear this mask," he said, slightly muffled, "I defend those who cannot defend themselves."

"A…witch?"

The witch nodded.

"Any special reason why?"

"It is unexpected. It is frightening. Nobody would ever guess it was me."

"Because it's a witch? No offense, Peter, but you aren't built like most people." Marcus was starting to believe that he should flee the car and take his chances outside.

"This was my mom's mask."

"For fighting crime?"

"No, for Halloween. But she's my hero, and to honor her, I wear it."

"So…what? You go around on a broomstick fighting crime?"

"You promised you wouldn't make fun of me."

"That wasn't making fun of you," Marcus insisted. "You're wearing a green warty witch mask. It was a legitimate question."

"You know perfectly well that I can't fly."

"I didn't say fly. I said, 'Go around.' You could be acting like you were flying on a broomstick but just walking around with it. I guess that does sound like I'm making fun of you, but you're the one wearing a witch mask."

"I'll accept that," said Peter. "I do not have a broom. I don't wear a pointy black hat or a cloak, and I don't have an eye of newt in my pocket. I don't stir a bubbling cauldron, and I don't try to cast spells. I did try to cackle once. But it sounded dumb, and I didn't try again. I wear this mask when I protect the defenseless."

Marcus didn't know if asking if Peter was joking would count as making fun of him. He decided not to risk it. "Okay, you're a superhero known as the Witch."

"I didn't say superhero."

"You implied it."

"I behave in a way that a superhero would, but I'd never use that word to describe myself. If I had Batman's funding, I might, but I don't. And I don't call myself the Witch. If others choose to do that, that's their business. I simply protect my secret identity so my mother isn't subjected to attempts by villains to seek vengeance. I come out here every once in a while to help keep the streets safe."

"Okay," said Marcus. "Well, this has been very eye-opening and educational. I'm honored that you trusted me with your secret, and you have my promise that I won't breathe a word about it to a single soul. I'm glad we went on this little adventure."

"I'm glad too."

"Ready to take off the ol' witch mask and go home? We need a good night's sleep if we're going to do school and shark tank construction and stuff tomorrow."

Peter reached down and pulled a lever to pop the trunk. "No way did we drive all the way out here not to stop a crime."

17

NOW MARCUS DECIDED that his question would not be considered making fun of Peter. "You're joking, right?"

"Nope."

"I'm not getting out of the car."

"I didn't say that *you* would be stopping crime. You're just going to watch while I do it." Peter opened the door.

"Seriously, Peter," said Marcus, staring to panic, "this isn't funny anymore."

"I won't let you get hurt."

"Look, I don't want to offend you by using the word delusional, but yes, you're being just a tiny bit delusional. You can't go fighting crime in a witch mask. You're going to get killed."

"I haven't died yet."

"Lots of people didn't die until the moment they got themselves killed."

Peter got out of the car. "C'mon."

"No."

"C'mon."

"No."

Peter shut the door and walked back to the trunk. He raised the lid.

This was absolute madness. This was pure, unfiltered insanity. People didn't do this! They didn't drive out to a scary part of town, put on a Halloween mask, and venture out to fight crime! It was not the traditional way that humans chose to behave!

Marcus needed to call Mom, tell her about his poor judgment, and ask her to pick him up. He was about to place the call, but then he flinched. A witch was standing next to the door. He had plenty of evidence that it was, in fact, Peter in his witch mask, but Marcus couldn't lie to himself. There'd been a split second when he thought it was a real witch.

"C'mon, Marcus. It'll be exciting." Peter held out a pair of hockey sticks, which seemed woefully inadequate for an evening of crime fighting.

"I don't want or need any more excitement in my life."

Peter tried to open the door, but it was locked. He pressed a button on his car key, unlocking the door, and then he opened it. "Are you calling the police?"

"No, my parents."

"Why?"

"To pick me up."

"Oh, you'd be dead long before they got here. Why is somebody who can fend off three big kids with a deck of cards so worried?"

"Ken, Chris, and Joe weren't going to shoot or stab me. Or both!"

"You don't know that."

"It's a reasonable assumption."

"I guess so." Peter scratched his cheek, but apparently, he couldn't get at the itch through the mask, so he reached underneath it.

"If you want to be a vigilante, that's totally fine," said Marcus. "I'm choosing a slightly different plan for tonight."

"Please don't," said Peter.

"Sorry. I'm not going to watch you put yourself in peril."

Peter lowered his head like a child being scolded. "I guess this was a bad idea."

"You think?"

Peter returned to the back of the car, put away the hockey sticks, and closed the trunk.

"Hello! What have we here?" somebody called out.

Marcus turned at the sound of the voice. It was two guys about a block away. One had spiky blond hair, and the other had shaggy blond hair. They looked a few years older than Marcus and Peter. Neither of them appeared to be particularly pleasant individuals.

"Oh, we've got some Halloween action going on!" said the shaggy one. "Looks like we're in the middle of a zombie attack!"

"I'm a witch," Peter muttered, but not loud enough for them to hear.

"Get in the car, Peter," said Marcus. "Get in the car really fast so we can drive away."

Marcus felt a little guilty for assuming that these guys were bad news. They might simply be delighted that somebody was in the holiday spirit.

They guys reached into their leather jackets. The spiky one took out a great big knife, and the shaggy one took out a claw hammer. Marcus felt less guilty.

"Peter! Car! Peter! Car!"

Peter climbed into the driver's seat and shut the door. "I know I can handle them, but I'll respect your wishes."

"Start the engine! Start the engine! Start it! Start it!"

Peter slid the key into the ignition and turned it. Marcus expected the car to start. It did not. The engine made a sound like it was kind of *trying* to roar to life, but it didn't actually turn over.

"Hmmmm," said Peter.

"Start it! Start it! Start it!"

Peter continued to twist the key, but the car still didn't start. Marcus glanced over at the guys, who looked very amused by their automotive difficulties. They weren't running toward the vehicle or even picking up their pace, but it was clear that the car was their destination.

"This has never happened before," said Peter.

"What did you do to the car?" Marcus demanded.

"I didn't do anything to the car!"

"You sabotaged it!"

"Why would I sabotage it?"

"Because you want to fight crime!"

"Yeah, but I want to be able to drive home afterward!"

"Start it!"

"Do *you* want to try?"

"Yes! I do!" Marcus leaned over and turned the key in the ignition. The engine made a noise that indicated it was aware of the basic concept of what was supposed to be happening, but it wasn't ready to commit.

"Don't twist it so hard!" said Peter. "You'll break the key!"

Marcus let go of the key and leaned back in his seat. He was getting tired of fearing for his personal safety. He just wanted to go for a short amount of time—perhaps two or three days— without being in danger. Two or three days. That was all.

"Please start your car," requested Marcus, keeping his voice calm.

"I'm sure it'll start this time," said Peter, turning the key again. The car didn't start. This time it didn't even make a noise to indicate that it was trying.

The two guys walked up to the car. The shaggy-haired guy

with the hammer stood next to Marcus's window, and the spiky-haired guy with the knife stood next to Peter's.

"Did you ever end up calling 911?" Peter asked.

"No."

"That's disappointing."

"Drop your phone on the floor," said Shaggy Hair. Marcus wasn't sure if the ruffian had heard Peter's question or if it just made sense that, as a criminal, he would know to address the phone issue on his own.

Marcus considered *not* dropping it, but at this point calling the police would just expedite the process of the two guys killing them, so he tossed his phone by his feet.

"Get out of the car," said Spiky Hair.

Peter and Marcus both shook their heads.

Shaggy Hair and Spiky Hair tested the door handles. Fortunately, they were locked, ensuring Marcus a couple of extra seconds of sweet, precious life.

"Unlock the door," said Shaggy Hair.

"Don't unlock the door," Marcus told Peter.

Shaggy Hair held up the hammer and tapped it gently against the window. "I said...unlock the door."

"Peter, I'll give you a million dollars if you tell me this is a practical joke," said Marcus.

"Do I have to tell the truth?"

"Yeah."

"I can't do that."

Shaggy Hair tapped his hammer against the glass again, less gently this time. "Don't make me come in there after you."

Peter said, "They could just be messing with us."

Shaggy Hair bashed the hammer into the window, shattering the glass. There was no need for Peter to say, "Well, I guess they aren't." They both understood that once the situation escalated to a car window being broken by a claw hammer, it was no longer likely to be an amusing prank.

Marcus wanted to stay brave, so he let out his bravest scream.

"Going to unlock the door now?" asked Shaggy Hair. The lock was now easily accessible to both of them, but Marcus reached over and pulled it up. Shaggy Hair thanked him and opened the door. "Get out."

Marcus decided that it was in his best interest to follow instructions. He got out of the car.

"Give me your wallet," said Shaggy Hair.

Marcus took his wallet out of his back pocket and handed it over. Shaggy Hair opened it up and flipped through the contents. "Eight bucks?"

"I thought it was nine."

"I miscounted. Nine bucks? It's barely worth breaking your window for nine bucks."

"Sorry."

"Where are your credit cards?"

"I'm fifteen."

"Don't you have, like, a movie theater gift card or something?

This frozen yogurt card only has two stamps on it." He took out Marcus's student ID and looked back and forth between it and Marcus. "Not a great picture, dude."

"I know."

"Does he have a library card?" asked Spiky Hair.

"Yeah."

"Maybe we could check out a bunch of books and sell them."

"Nah. The libraries are all closed. He'll cancel the card before they open tomorrow." Shaggy Hair took out the nine dollars, shoved it into his pocket, and tossed the wallet back at Marcus. "You made me waste my time, kid. Know what I do to people who waste my time?"

Marcus shook his head.

"Guess."

"I don't know."

"Try anyway."

"You scold them?"

"Nope."

"Tickle them?"

Shaggy Hair held the hammer up to Marcus's face. "What I do is I knock out all of their teeth. So yeah, it's the same punishment as if you hadn't gotten out of the car."

"Do you want to see a magic trick?" Marcus asked.

"What?"

"I'm a magician. Do you want to see a card trick?"

"Nope, I sure don't."

"It'll only take a minute."

"Are you seriously trying to distract me from knocking out your teeth by offering to show me a magic trick?"

"No, I'm offering some entertainment. Without teeth, I can't really do my patter, so it'll be my last trick for a while."

"Are you hearing this?" Shaggy Hair asked Spiky Hair. "The kid is trying to distract me with a trick. Nobody would be dumb enough to fall for that."

"These three bullies were threatening to beat me up, and it worked on them," Marcus offered.

"No way."

"It did."

"The bullies at your school must not be very smart."

"Bullies usually aren't."

"Didn't they suspect that something was up? If I'm about to mug somebody and they offer to do a magic trick, I automatically assume that their intentions are sneaky."

"I'm sure they thought I was being sneaky," said Marcus, "but they got caught up in the performance."

"But why did they even let you begin? That's the part I'm having a problem with."

"I guess you had to be there."

"I can't envision that scenario. If I'm going to punch somebody or break their bones with a hammer, there's no way that I'd ever allow them to start a magic trick. Don't get me wrong. I enjoy magic as much as anybody. Well, maybe a little less than most people, but I still enjoy it on occasion. If I'm at one of my nephew or niece's birthday parties and a magician comes out, it's not like I leave the room or anything. But it's a completely different environment. It doesn't make sense."

"Like I said, you had to be there."

"Who were these bullies? Give me their names. If they're that dumb, maybe I should pay them a visit, get them out of the gene pool."

Marcus didn't think Shaggy Hair was serious, but he also didn't want three dead seniors on his conscience. "Abner, Hugo, and Mortimer."

"What are their last names?"

"I'm not sure. I don't know them very well."

"That's okay. This will be more of a challenge. I'm always looking for ways to pass the time."

"So you're going to hunt down the bullies and let us go?" Marcus asked.

"Oh, no, no, I hope I didn't give you that idea. Apologies if I did. It certainly wasn't my intention."

"You're going to kill us?"

"Nah."

"You're going to insult us and then let us go?"

"Worse than that."

"You're going to…shove me?"

Shaggy Hair grinned. "Magicians use their hands a lot, don't they?"

"Yes," Marcus confirmed.

"You use your hands to shuffle cards, to make coins disappear, to wave magic wands—all that stuff. Could you be an effective magician without the use of your hands?"

Marcus felt a full-fledged panic attack coming on. "Not really."

Shaggy Hair scraped the claw end of his hammer down the side of Peter's car. "Yeah, it would be a bummer if something happened to your hands."

Marcus said nothing.

For the first time since the hooligans had broken the windows, Peter spoke up, "If you hurt him, I'll destroy you."

Shaggy Hair glanced over at him. "That so?"

"Yes."

"Planning to eat my brains?"

"It's a witch mask, not a zombie."

"Fine. Planning to cast a spell on me?"

"Perhaps."

"Take off the mask."

"No. Sorry."

"My buddy has a really big knife, and I think you'll be unpleasantly surprised by how willing he is to use it. My recommendation—and it's just a recommendation—is that you do exactly what we tell you to do when we tell you to do it. If you choose to ignore that, well, we make our own choices in life, I suppose."

Shaggy Hair returned his attention to Marcus. "Put out your hand."

"No."

"I strongly suggest that you put out your hand."

"What are you going to do?" Marcus asked.

"I'm going to make it more difficult for you to do magic tricks."

"Please don't."

"Asking nicely won't help. You have three seconds."

This had to be a prank. It had to be. Marcus really wanted Peter to be so desperate for attention that he was willing to pay somebody to break his car windows to impress Marcus. The possibility simply did not exist that Marcus was actually standing in a shady part of town with some guy demanding he put out his hand so that he could crush it. This couldn't be happening. No way. Not a chance. Not in the real world.

"Three...two..."

Marcus put out his left hand, palm up.

"Thank you," said Shaggy Hair. "I bet you think I'm the kind of person who's too nice to do something really terrible. Maybe you're right. Let's see, shall we?"

Marcus just stood there. His hand quivered in fear. His entire body was shaking too. He felt like even his veins were trembling in terror.

Shaggy Hair winked. Then he raised the hammer over his head and slammed it down on Marcus's hand.

18

IF IT HAD turned out to be a foam hammer, Marcus would have laughed and laughed and laughed. "Good one!" he would've said. "You totally got me!"

It was not a foam hammer.

If it had been a rubber hammer, Marcus also would have laughed and laughed and laughed. "I thought it was a real hammer!" he would have said, wiping tears of merriment from his eyes. "Oh, what a fun-filled, lighthearted joke you've played on me! For the next few decades, whenever I'm feeling a bit sad, I'll look back upon this moment, and it will immediately cheer me up!"

It was not a rubber hammer.

Nor was it made from very thin plastic, which might have harmlessly shattered upon striking Marcus's hand. Nor was it made from soft squishy clay. Nor was it made from duck feathers that had been molded into the shape of a hammer.

It was a real steel hammer.

The head of the hammer did not pop off in the nick of time. The hammer did not slip out of Shaggy Hair's hand an instant before impact. It did not harmlessly bounce off of Marcus's palm and smack Shaggy Hair in the face. Nobody flung a lasso around it and yanked it away.

No, a real metal hammer bashed into Marcus's hand. It hurt so badly that he dropped to his knees, crying out in pain.

Was his hand broken?

It might be.

Was Shaggy Hair going to finish the job?

He might.

It was hard for Marcus to keep track of what happened next because he was shrieking "Aaahhhh!" so frequently. He thought he heard the trunk pop open, and he thought he heard a car door open. He thought he heard Spiky Hair make an *oomph* sound as if he'd been struck by a car door, and he thought he heard something metal like a large knife clatter to the ground. But he couldn't verify any of these sounds because his eyes were squeezed shut as he screamed.

But Marcus definitely heard both Spiky Hair and Shaggy Hair say extremely unkind things, and then he heard some commotion and sounds that could have conceivably been generated by hockey sticks smacking against bodies multiple times. Other sounds included but weren't limited to the noises a pair of guys might make when they dropped unconscious as a result of being repeatedly struck with a hockey stick.

"Marcus?"

Marcus looked up at Peter, who was still wearing the witch mask. He held a broken hockey stick. Shaggy Hair lay motionless next to him, and since there was no sign of Spiky Hair, he was presumably lying on the other side of the car.

"How—"

"Are you okay?"

"What—"

"How's your hand?"

"Huh?"

And then everything went black.

~~~~

"Marcus? Hey, Marcus! Wake up!"

Marcus opened his eyes. "How long was I out?"

"You just hit the ground. A second and a half maybe?"

"Okay, good." Marcus cried out again in pain. He'd never known that being hit in the hand with a hammer could hurt so much. He had never entertained the thought that it might be a *pleasant* sensation, but this was at least 35 percent more painful than he would have predicted.

"How's your hand?"

"Didn't you just hear me scream?"

Peter crouched down next to him. "It doesn't look broken."

"You can't see that through my skin."

"At least he didn't use the claw part."

"Yes, everything is simply wonderful."

"Can you move your fingers?"

"There's one that I'll be happy to move," Marcus snapped.

"Seriously, can you move them?"

Marcus wiggled his fingers. It hurt like crazy, but his fingers seemed okay. His palm was starting to swell.

"I'm really sorry," said Peter. "I thought I had this under control." He gestured to Shaggy Hair. "I mean, I *did* have it under control, just not before he hammered your hand."

"We should run. Let me get my phone. And could you take off that mask? It's creeping me out."

"If they wake up, they'll know my secret identity."

"Are you kidding me? Peter, you're not a superhero!"

"The two unconscious villains would disagree."

"I won't lie. I'm impressed that you knocked them out. But you're a high school freshman in a witch mask holding a hockey stick. We're not in a comic book or a TV show or a big-budget movie or a video game or a web series or any of the made-up places where superheroes exist! Whatever issues you're working out are none of my business, but because of you, I have to make a shark disappear with a broken hand, so forgive me if I'm not calling you the Amazing Peter Chumlin!"

"Chumkin."

"Whatever."

"You don't even know my name?"

"I was close!"

"I revealed my secret identity, and you don't even know my name?" Peter sounded heartbroken even through the rubber mask.

"You didn't reveal your secret identity. Your secret identity by definition is your *real* identity. I already knew that. You revealed your superhero identity."

"You know what I meant."

"I don't know what anything means right now! I've never been so confused in my life! There's a giant vortex of confusion swirling around my head! And I apologize for getting your last name slightly wrong. I got it right when I told my friend Kimberly about you. But I'm still reacting to my broken hand, so cut me some slack!"

"I really don't think it's broken."

"Unless one of your superpowers is X-ray vision, you don't get to tell me if my hand is broken or not!" Marcus was so frustrated and angry that he wanted to punch something. Of course, that would only worsen the situation. He reached into the car and picked up his cell phone. "And you're not helping me do the trick anymore."

Peter pulled off the witch mask. "What do you mean?"

"What do you think I mean? We're done! I can't trust you to be around a shark."

"I saved your life!" said Peter. "How do you know he wasn't going to bash in your head next?"

"You put me in this situation in the first place!"

"You came along willingly!"

"No, I protested the entire time!"

Peter thought for a moment. "Yeah, I guess you did. I just thought that once you saw me defend justice, you'd…I don't know—"

"I don't know either. I have no idea what you were thinking. Why are we still standing around talking? They could wake up any second."

"If they did, I'd just knock them out again. It's not that difficult once they're already on the ground."

"Let's go."

"You're not going anywhere," said a sinister but familiar voice. Seamus was standing on the other side of the car.

"How did you get here?" Marcus demanded. He was so angry that he forgot he should be frightened for his life.

"Magic."

"Seriously, how did you get here?"

"I followed you, of course. I had no other plans for this

evening. My social calendar is light these days. Bingo on Sunday nights, but that's about it. And yes, I cheat at bingo."

Marcus didn't ask how he cheated at bingo. Some other time he might have been interested, but right now he didn't care. Seamus stood there as if waiting for Marcus to ask how he cheated, but when Marcus said nothing, he shrugged and dropped the subject.

"Who are you, and how did you follow us?" asked Peter.

"My name is Sinister Seamus. Your friend knows and fears me. I'm not a master private investigator, but I've followed people in their automobiles on a few occasions. I was wondering why you would travel to such an unsavory destination. I'm still wondering."

"Me too," said Marcus. "It's a long, baffling story."

Shaggy Hair let out a groan.

"We need to get out of here before he wakes up," said Marcus.

"I'm not quite ready to flee yet," said Seamus. "We'll have to subdue him again. Your name is Peter, right?"

Peter nodded.

"You're the one who knocked them out the first time, and since you clearly have your technique down, it makes sense that you'd do it a second time. You'd be re-knocking them out to protect your friend and to serve justice. If I did it, it'd be because I like to hit people. Which reason should we go with?"

"Uh, it doesn't matter to me."

"Perhaps we should make Marcus do it?"

"I vote we run," said Marcus.

"I vote we run too," said Peter.

"Here's how it will work," said Seamus. "For every human being you have killed, you get one vote. Marcus, how many people have you killed? On purpose or by accident, it doesn't matter."

"None."

"Really? Fifteen years old and you haven't killed a single person? What have you been doing with your life all this time?"

Shaggy Hair started to push himself up.

"Peter, same question," said Seamus. "Let me know if you need me to repeat it."

"None," said Peter.

"You don't even sound ashamed of that."

"I guess I'm not."

"Both of you have squandered your lives. We can't all be killing people by the age of three like me, but fifteen? That's just plain lazy."

"Who is this guy again?" Peter asked Marcus.

"If Marcus is in a squeamish mood, I suppose I'll have to step up to the plate," said Seamus. "That's a baseball reference. A hockey reference would be more appropriate, but I'm not that familiar with the sport. Do you have a reference I could use, Peter?"

"Uh, time to skate out onto the ice?"

"I suppose I'll have to skate out onto the ice." Seamus kicked Shaggy Hair in the head, and he flopped back onto the ground, motionless. "Oh, I enjoyed that. I'm going to do it again, even though it's unnecessary." Seamus kicked him twice more.

"Can we go now?" asked Marcus.

"We cannot," said Seamus. "I may have misheard, but if I'm not mistaken, you told your friend that he would not be participating in your illusion. Is that correct?"

"Yeah," said Marcus, holding up his swollen hand.

"In the world of magic, there is nothing more important than loyalty. Perhaps it's misplaced loyalty in this scenario. Your friend caused a punk to break your hand because he took you into a terrible part of town, all because of his delusional belief that he's a superhero. Still, misplaced or not, I reject your effort to cut him loose."

"What?" asked Marcus.

"In the world of magic, there is nothing more important than—"

"I heard you."

"I must have misunderstood what you meant by *what*."

"Are you saying I have to work with him?"

"Bingo!"

"He almost got me killed. He still might!"

"Yes, he's not an ideal partner. You should have chosen better before you saved him from bullies."

"How do you know everything?"

"Like I said, light social calendar."

"He didn't save me," said Peter. "I was protecting my secret identity."

"Also," said Seamus, "because of your attempt at disloyalty, I'm cutting one month off your deadline."

"What?"

"In the world of magic, there is nothing more important than—"

"I heard you," said Marcus. "But you can't do that!"

"Of course I can," said Seamus. "I can also order you not to tell the police, your parents, or any medical professionals what really happened to your hand. You'll have to make something up. Something interesting but not too interesting."

"I can't do the trick in a month," Marcus insisted. "I probably couldn't do it in two months! It's gone from ridiculous and impossible to ridiculouser and impossibler. I mean, more ridiculous and more impossible! This isn't fair!"

"Life isn't fair," said Seamus. "In life, sometimes you get the middle seat on a plane and sometimes your selfies get photobombed. Deal with it."

"You've already printed the posters."

"I'll print new ones. When you reach my level of sheer evil, you don't care about the paper waste." Seamus frowned. "I mean, obviously I'll put the old ones in a recycling bin. It's important to take care of the environment."

"If you're making it impossible for me to do the trick, I might as well call the police."

"I wouldn't."

"I will."

"I wouuuuuuuuuuldn't," said Seamus, singing his words.

"Evil people suck," said Marcus. "I just want to throw that out there."

"Noted," said Seamus. "So let's recap. You have one less month to prepare your astounding illusion. You are required to work closely with Peter, even though he's proven himself to be unstable. You are also required to work closely with Kimberly, because she seems quite delightful."

"Hey, I think I hear the other guy moaning," said Peter. "Do you want to whack him again, or should I? Or should we leave now?"

"You go ahead and whack him."

"All right." Peter went around to the other side of the car. There was a loud whack followed by a groan from Spiky Hair, and then Peter rejoined Marcus and Seamus.

"Is he dead?" Seamus asked.

"No, no, just sleeping."

"A pity. Is there anything else we need to discuss?"

"Nah," said Marcus. "I think we're good."

"Okay. Well, I don't know about you two, but I've had a most enjoyable evening. I'm sure I've had more fun than you two, but that's because I'm evil."

"You keep talking about how evil you are," said Peter. "A truly evil person wouldn't need to keep saying it to everybody."

"Do you want me to demonstrate it instead of saying it?"

"No, that's okay."

"Are we finally done?" asked Marcus.

"Almost," said Seamus. "I'm also a pretty good mechanic. Pop the hood, and let's see what I can do."

19

MARCUS AND PETER drove away. Seamus had indeed fixed the car, though he kept threatening to kill them while he was doing it.

"I'm sorry about all of this," said Peter. "I shouldn't have put us in danger."

"No, you really shouldn't have."

"I'm trying to apologize."

"I get that. Nobody has ever needed to apologize to me more."

"I'm sorry."

"I don't accept your apology."

"You have to accept an apology."

"I have to accept an apology if you spill soup on my shirt. I don't have to accept one if you get my hand broken."

"I'm still going to make you a great shark tank."

"Oh, gosh, yay."

"I guess we need a cover story," said Peter.

"We were building a mock-up of the tank using wooden boards. You were hammering in a nail and hit my hand instead."

"That makes me sound clumsy."

"Too bad."

"It doesn't make you sound all that great either. You shouldn't have your hand on a board if people are hammering nails into it."

"Do you have a better idea?"

"I figured a hammer fell off a shelf onto your hand."

"That sounds like a lie. Why would a hammer fall off a shelf?"

"Earthquake?"

"No."

"Maybe I accidentally bumped the shelf," Peter suggested. "That still makes me sound clumsy, but it's not as bad as me accidentally hitting your hand."

"That's completely… Actually, yeah, that makes sense."

"What about the car windows?"

"We found them like that."

"Wow, you're a good liar. But I guess that's what magicians do."

"No," said Marcus. "Magicians deceive people who know they're being deceived. When a magician goes up on stage to perform a trick, it's understood by everybody in the audience that there's an illusion involved. That's the whole point. This isn't the same thing at all."

"Sorry. I didn't realize you were so sensitive about it."

"Now you know."

Peter nervously drummed his fingers on the steering wheel. "So, uh, this is going to sound crazy, but we don't have to make up a cover story. What I mean is that we could just keep driving wherever the road takes us. That Seamus guy can't follow us forever."

"What are you talking about?"

"Leaving all our problems behind. Drive away."

"Are you out of your mind? Don't answer that. I already know."

"We wouldn't have to worry about dying or making a shark disappear. It's win-win."

"I don't think you understand what win-win means," said Marcus.

"I'm not saying it would be an easy life, but there would be no homework, no tests, no psycho magicians. At least think about it."

Marcus gaped at him. "Do you really for one fraction of a split millisecond believe that I'm going to leave my parents, leave school, leave my entire *life* so we can drive around the country? Do you really think I would take you up on that offer?"

"I guess not," said Peter.

"Every time I think you can't get weirder, you get weirder. And though I like weirdness, that's not a compliment."

"I'm sorry. It was a bad suggestion."

"Yes, it was."

"I guess you have more to stick around for than I do."

"Like trying to pull off a spectacular illusion or get killed by a madman if I mess it up. I'm not happy about the situation, but I'm certainly not going to just drive off. I thought you said your mom was your hero?"

"She is. I don't know what I was saying." Peter was quiet for a moment. "Sorry."

"Stop talking. Just take me to the hospital."

〜〜〜

"It's not broken," said Dr. Webber, pointing to an X-ray. "Keep the ice pack on it, and the swelling will go down. You'll be okay in a few days."

"Thanks," said Marcus. Mom and Dad were in the room with him. Nobody questioned the idea that a hammer had fallen off a shelf and hit his hand, but he supposed there was no reason for anybody to think he'd made up a cover story.

"Hammers are dangerous beasts," said Dr. Webber. "I've never trusted them."

"Seriously?"

"No, that was a joke. I suppose that's why I became a

doctor instead of a stand-up comedian. Just trying to bring a little levity into a generally unpleasant experience. I never imagined that you'd take me at my word. I apologize."

"I'm just stressed out, I guess," said Marcus.

"Well, of course. You were attacked by a hammer." Dr. Webber smiled. "Now before you go getting yourself worked up, that was another joke. I try to perform at the open mic at the Wacky Chuckle Farm on Wednesdays whenever I'm not too busy."

"I'm sure you're very amusing," said Dad.

"Obviously, I use better material than the hammer thing. That was just an ad-lib. I'll refine it a bit for the next time somebody comes in here with a hammer injury."

"It's fine the way you said it," said Marcus and sighed.

"You think so? Thanks. I appreciate that."

~~~

"You've had a rough few days," said Mom as they drove home. "Grandpa Zachary passed away, and now you hurt your hand. Things can't get much worse."

"Nope," said Marcus.

"So this Peter, is he always that clumsy?"

"I guess. I don't know him that well."

"I'm not sure you should be hanging out with kids who bump into shelves," Mom said.

"He's fine."

"What will he bump into next? You're lucky it was only a hammer on that shelf and not a chainsaw."

"A lot of kids are clumsy at that age," Dad said. "Give him a break. And I don't think Marcus is entirely blameless here."

"What do you mean?" asked Marcus.

Dad glanced up at him in the rearview mirror. "Your reflexes are too fast to get hit by a falling hammer. You were trying to catch it, weren't you?"

"Yes, sir," Marcus admitted, figuring, *Hey, why not?*

"It's understandable. In the moment you see something fall, your first instinct is to reach out and catch it. Sometimes it works out for you like if it was a hamster, and sometimes it doesn't like if it was a hammer. Unfortunately, tonight you got the hammer."

20

THE NEXT DAY at school, it was difficult for Marcus to concentrate. He gave wildly incorrect answers to every question he was asked. He even gave a biology-related answer to a history question, and everybody started laughing at him.

At lunchtime he sat outside again, hoping to avoid Peter. He felt too sick to his stomach to eat anything, so he just sat there, wallowing in good old-fashioned self-pity.

Peter came around the corner of the school and saw Marcus sitting on the bench. His mouth opened as if he were going to say something, but then he seemed to realize that Marcus was not in the mood for conversation. His closed his mouth and left.

For the rest of the day, Marcus continued to give remarkably unintelligent answers to the questions his teachers asked, including the most incorrect usage of the word hypotenuse ever uttered. His teachers seemed to realize how distracted he was because they called on him five times more often than usual.

Between classes he tried to relax himself by shuffling cards, but he ended up dropping the entire deck on the floor.

"Hur-hur, wanna play fifty-two pickup?" asked some kid walking past.

Marcus gathered up his cards and wondered if his stomach would ever stop hurting. It felt as if he'd eaten seventeen slices of pizza with triple grease and a six-inch-high pile of jalapenos on top, except without the enjoyment of actually eating any pizza.

How difficult was it to fake one's death and move to another country under a different name? He'd never heard of anybody successfully accomplishing this, but of course, he'd only hear about it if they got caught. In theory, hundreds of people faked their own deaths every day. It would be the ultimate illusion.

Marcus knew he wouldn't be faking his own death and moving to New Zealand, but it felt good to think about it for a few moments.

At the merciful sound of the final bell, Marcus got his books from his locker and walked down the hallway. He had the daunting fear a shark might burst through the tile floor at any moment, biting him in half, but that was probably an irrational fear.

As he walked out of the building, he heard Peter call out, "Hey, Marcus!"

And then Kimberly also said, "Hey, Marcus!"

He turned around. Both of them were coming toward him from slightly different directions. Peter reached him first.

"I really need to apologize," said Peter.

Kimberly joined them a couple of seconds later. "Sorry to interrupt," she said, "but I really need to apologize."

"No, you don't," said Marcus.

"Yes, I do," said Peter.

"*You* do, for sure," said Marcus. He looked at Kimberly. "You don't."

"I think I should." She looked at Peter. "By the way, I'm Kimberly. Hi."

"Hi," said Peter. "I'm Peter."

"It's been eating away at me all day," said Kimberly.

"You already apologized a bunch of times."

"I know, but I wanted to apologize after some time had passed, so you knew it was sincere. But I probably shouldn't be apologizing in front of your new friend because that'd make everything even weirder, but apparently, I've lost my ability to interact with people without making it weird."

"Do you want me to go?" asked Peter.

"No," said Kimberly.

"Yes," said Marcus.

"I don't know who I should listen to," said Peter.

"Me," said Marcus.

"Me," said Kimberly. "You don't need to go. I'm not here to interrupt whatever you two were talking about. I came over here to say I'm sorry, and I did it, even though it was kind of long-winded, and now I'm heading off to orchestra practice, so you two can return to your conversation and pretend I never interrupted."

"Fine," said Marcus. "Thank you for apologizing. We're okay now, right?"

Kimberly nodded. "Yes."

"Hey, Magic Boy," said a voice that Marcus desperately hoped didn't belong to Ken but sounded exactly like him. Ken, flanked by his best buddies Joe and Chris, walked over to them. "Where do you think you're going?"

"Home," said Marcus.

"Is that so?"

"Yes."

"Oh." Ken frowned, apparently having expected some sort of sarcastic response that he could get angry about. "You can't go yet."

"Are you going to beat me up here right in front of the school?" Marcus asked.

"Nah, I figured we'd walk off school property first."

"Not going to happen," said Marcus.

"What are you going to do? Live at school? Eat scraps from the lunchroom?"

"You could eat them out of Peter's hair," Chris volunteered. He and Joe both laughed hysterically.

"Aw, man, that was a knee-slapper!" said Joe, slapping his own knee.

"Did you just call it a knee-slapper and then slap your knee?" Ken asked.

Joe frowned. "Yeah. I mean, should I not have?"

"If you want to command any respect in this school, you don't use the phrase knee-slapper in response to a joke. It's one of the least cool things you can do. When you add actually slapping your knee to the mix, I don't even want to associate with you anymore."

"I was doing it ironically."

"I don't think you were."

"No, seriously, it was total irony. I would never have done something like that if it weren't, uh, you know, social commentary."

"Go away," said Ken. "We're done."

"I'm out of the group?"

"Yes."

Joe looked to Chris for help. "Are you going to let him do this to me?"

"I...I think it might be kind of extreme, but you have to admit that your reaction to my joke *was* pretty embarrassing."

"You've said 'knee-slapper' before! I've heard you! And it wasn't all that long ago!"

"But I didn't say it in front of Ken!"

"So? It happened! You still said it!"

"I didn't actually slap my knee. I think that's the most important element."

"I was being ironic!"

"You're saying that retroactively. In the moment you were speaking and acting from the heart."

"Fine," said Joe. "I don't need you guys. I've got other friends."

"No, you don't," said Chris.

"I've got friends all over the place." He pointed and waved at somebody walking by. "That was a friend right there. I just don't talk to him very much because I spend so much time hanging out with you guys. See that girl over there? Friend. Total friend. More than a friend, if you get my meaning."

"Then why are you always with us instead of your girlfriend?" asked Chris.

"Because I thought you guys were cool. I was wrong. All these years I misjudged you two. Good-bye."

"Good-bye," said Chris.

Joe began to walk away and then turned back around. "Please don't banish me! I have no one else!"

"This has been fun, but I have to go to practice my cello now," said Kimberly.

"Don't go yet," said Marcus. "They'll stop talking soon, I promise."

"I want my marbles back," Joe told Chris.

"What marbles?"

"The ones I let you borrow that one time."

"We haven't played marbles since we were eight!"

"Yeah, and I want them back! There was a blue clear one and a lopsided one and an orange one."

"I don't have those anymore."

"You threw away my marbles?"

"Years ago."

"Why would you do that? Why wouldn't you return them to me?"

"Because they're marbles!" said Chris. "I didn't know you were obsessed with them."

"Now that our friendship is over, I want them back. And you know how we keep a bag of those circus peanuts in the cupboard at my house even though nobody in my house likes them? I'm throwing them away."

"I hate those things," said Chris.

"No, you don't."

"I only ate them to be polite."

"I've seen you eat an entire bag in less than a minute!"

"Yeah, I was feeling really polite that day."

"You're lying to me about circus peanuts!" said Joe. "What's happened to us?"

Chris shrugged and avoided eye contact.

"I'll go now," said Joe. "I take back every high-five we ever exchanged."

Joe walked away, his head hanging low.

"I don't remember what we were talking about before," said Ken.

"We were going to beat him up," said Chris, pointing to Marcus.

"That's right."

Marcus held up his gauze-covered hand. "I can't fight right now," he said.

"Oh, wow, did that happen when you punched Ken?" asked Chris.

That was an excellent question. The best answer was not necessarily the truthful one. Peter wouldn't correct him if he said, "Why, yes, I acquired this injury whilst punching Kenneth as punishment for his bullying behavior," but it would be a lie. He should tell the truth.

Or should he?

Yeah, he should.

"Nah," he said. "It happened after that."

"You'd better clear out," said Kimberly. "His other hand is fine, and he might break that one on the *other* side of your face."

"My face?" asked Ken. "He never punched me in the face."

Marcus squirmed a bit as he realized that this discussion might not end in his favor.

21

"I THOUGHT YOU punched him?" Kimberly asked Marcus.

"He did," said Chris. "Right in the gut. You should've seen Ken hit the ground! Wham! Thud!" Chris laughed and then started to lift his arm to high-five Joe but then remembered that he'd left.

"Oh," said Kimberly. "That's not how I was led to believe it happened."

Marcus continued to squirm. He wasn't sure how much trouble he might be in. He had indeed won the fight with Ken (if you could call it an actual fight), so it wasn't as if he said, "Oh, yeah, I *destroyed* him!" when in fact he'd run off with his tail between his legs, going "Yip! Yip! Yip!" On the other hand, he'd known when he was telling the story to Kimberly that admitting to a sucker punch might make him look bad. And even if it didn't, now he'd entered dicey territory. *It's not about what happened. It's that you lied about it.*

"He took out a deck of cards and started doing a trick," said Chris. "And then at the moment when Ken was least expecting it, *whammo!* Right in the gut!"

"Whammo is just as bad as knee-slapper," said Ken.

"Stop trying to judge everyone's vocabulary."

Ken rolled his eyes. "Anyway, I'm just saying he hit me when I wasn't prepared for it. If it sounds like he was being all brave and stuff, he wasn't. It was a cowardly move. It wasn't anything he should be bragging about. I'd be ashamed of myself if I punched somebody in the stomach when they weren't expecting it. I'd have to make up a different story about what happened because there's no honor in that. None at all."

"In my defense," said Marcus, "there were three of you. I had to use my wits."

"That wasn't wits," said Ken. "That was being sneaky and unsportsmanlike."

Marcus wanted to say something about how it wasn't particularly sportsmanlike for them to pick on him and Peter in the first place, and he wanted to compare himself to a little-known sports team with no resources and compare Ken to an extremely popular and well-funded sports team too. Unfortunately, Marcus didn't know any sports teams well enough to be sure he didn't embarrass himself with his analogy.

"I disagree," he said instead.

"Disagree all you want," said Ken. "But you didn't do anything impressive. It was no great feat. Anybody can win a fight with a sucker punch."

"Anyway," said Kimberly, "I'm heading off. Enjoy the rest of your conflict."

Kimberly walked back to the main school entrance. Marcus wanted to go after her, but there really wasn't much he could say at this point except to offer her the opportunity to bash him over the head with her cello. (She would decline, of course, though she might use the bow. And she didn't have the cello with her anyway, so she'd have to go inside, retrieve a rather heavy instrument, carry it back out here, and then bash him with it, which was hopefully too much trouble to bother doing.)

"What was her deal?" asked Ken.

"Nothing," said Marcus.

"She seemed mad."

"Nah."

"It was like she was disappointed in you or something."

"Mind your own business."

Should he have said that? The expression on Ken's face seemed to indicate that Marcus should not have.

"You think you can talk to me like that?" Ken asked. He pointed to Peter. "He's sure not going to stick up for you."

Peter looked at the ground. Marcus had this horrifying

vision of Peter putting on his mask and shouting, "This looks like a job for…Witch-Man!" and then springing into action. Neither of them would ever live that down. It would haunt them until the end of their existence. Fortunately, instead of revealing his superhero identity to the world, Peter continued to stare at the ground.

"If you need revenge, go for it," Marcus told Ken. "I can't stop you. But I've got an injured hand. If you're the kind of person who would beat up somebody when they've got an injured hand, well, that tells all of the kids who are watching us everything they need to know."

Ken glanced around. A bunch of kids *were* watching them. For his own sanity, Marcus assumed that they were all hoping for a peaceful resolution.

"Hmmmm," said Ken. His brow furrowed. His eyes glazed over. Marcus guessed that Ken's mind was like a website that was taking a long time to load.

Ken stopped furrowing his brow and blinked. "I'm okay with people knowing that I'd beat up a kid with a hurt hand," he said. "But we can't do it on school property."

"Then I'm not leaving school property."

"You have to eventually," said Ken.

"I think we already covered this," said Chris. "That's when I made the comment about eating scraps of cafeteria food out of Peter's hair."

"Look, I can't keep dealing with you," Marcus told Ken.

"Like I said the last time you threatened me, I've got too much going on right now. What'll it take to satisfy you? Do I have to go to the hospital, or do you just need to get in one good punch?"

"I don't want you to go to the hospital," said Ken. "That would cause a lot of problems on my end. So yeah, I guess all I really want is one good punch."

"Face or gut?"

"To be fair, it would have to be a gut punch. It still wouldn't be completely fair because you'd be expecting it and you'd have a chance to tense your muscles, but it'd be fair enough that I'd stop coming after you."

"Okay," said Marcus. "I let you punch me in the stomach, and you leave me and Peter alone for the rest of the school year. Do we have a deal?"

"The end of the school year is pretty far away," Ken noted. "I can't commit to that."

"I'm not going to let you punch me if you're going to do it again a week from now."

"It wouldn't be a week. What if we went until holiday break? That gives you almost two months."

Marcus shook his head. "It's not even a month and a half. Spring break at the earliest."

"Spring break? That's not an option. Sorry. How about Groundhog Day?" asked Ken. "February 2. That's fair, right?"

"How about this? If the groundhog sees his shadow, you

can start bugging me again on Groundhog Day. If he doesn't and we have six more weeks of winter, you have to wait those six weeks."

"You've got it mixed up," said Chris. "The six more weeks of winter is if he sees his shadow, not if he doesn't see it."

"You sure?"

"Yeah."

"I don't think that's right," said Marcus. "If he sees his shadow, then the sun is out, so that would imply that the weather is getting better, not worse. It doesn't make sense."

"Yeah, but we're talking about a rodent sticking its head out of a hole to predict the changing of the seasons," Chris pointed out.

"I understand that. There still needs to be basic logic though."

Chris said, "I am 100 percent positive that if he sees his shadow, it means six more weeks of winter. I'll take the punch for Ken if I'm wrong."

"I think he's right," Peter told Marcus. "His shadow means six more weeks of winter."

"But that doesn't make sense," Marcus insisted.

Marcus, Peter, Chris, and Ken each took out their cell phones to research the subject. A few moments later, Chris and Peter were smiling, Marcus was frowning, and Ken was still reading the screen.

"Okay, well, I stand corrected," said Marcus. "If the

groundhog *does* see his shadow, you have to wait another six weeks before you can start bugging me again."

"No deal," said Ken. "Too complicated."

"Then why did you let us talk about it that long?"

"Here's my offer. Take it or leave it. One punch, and then I won't bother you until January 15. I think that's totally fair."

"January 21," Marcus countered.

"January 19."

"January 20."

"January 15."

"You can't go back to the fifteenth after you've offered the nineteenth."

"I can do whatever I want," said Ken. "I'm the one with the fist."

"No deal."

"I'm negotiating because I'm a reasonable guy, but technically, I can punch you in the stomach whenever I want."

"Okay," said Marcus. "January 19."

"January 15."

"January 17."

"Deal," said Ken.

Peter looked up from the ground. "I offer my stomach in Marcus's place."

"What?" Ken asked.

"You can punch me instead. As hard as you want."

"Nah."

"I think that's a great offer," said Marcus. "You get to quench your thirst for vengeance, and you get credit for punching a much larger person."

"Can't do it," said Ken. "The deal was to punch Magic Boy."

"Just offering," said Peter, looking down at the ground again.

Ken extended his hand to Marcus. "Shake on it?"

Marcus couldn't believe that he was about to do a hand-shake agreement that involved getting punched in the gut. But he needed at least one of his problems to go away, or else he'd go absolutely mad.

As he raised his hand, he noticed Bernard standing in the parking lot. Bernard looked extremely angry, and he was hold-ing up a poster. Marcus couldn't see it clearly from where he stood, but he was pretty sure this poster reflected the new date.

And that's when Marcus decided he'd had quite enough.

22

MARCUS LOWERED HIS hand.

"We didn't shake yet," said Ken.

Marcus reached into his pocket and took out a deck of cards. "Want to see a trick?"

"Uh-uh. No way. We aren't doing that again."

"You sure? It's a great trick. Watch." Marcus dropped the cards onto the ground. "See? The miracle of gravity! Want to see it again?"

"No."

Marcus took out another deck of cards. "Watch carefully." He dropped the cards. "Gravity! Science! Let's all give it up for science!" He ignored the pain in his left hand as he applauded for science. Nobody else joined in.

"How about another card trick?" he asked, reaching into his pocket. Alas, he had no more decks of cards. Marcus patted his other pocket and then patted the first pocket again in case he'd missed one. He patted the second pocket, and then he shrugged. "Guess I made all of my cards disappear! Ta-da!"

He applauded again, not caring how many of his fellow students were staring at him. Ken and Chris each took a tentative step backward as if they were concerned that Marcus might start biting people at random.

"How about a coin trick?" Marcus asked. "Everybody likes coin tricks!" He took a few coins out of his pocket and held up a nickel. "See this nickel?" He flicked it into the air. "Gone! See this quarter?" He flicked it into the air as well. "Gone! Oh, look. It's another nickel! Gone! I'm a magical genius! I bet none of you have any idea how I accomplished that amazing trick! Applaud!"

Nobody applauded. Several of the onlookers also stepped back.

Marcus threw all of his coins into the air. "All of them have magically disappeared! It's the most astounding illusion any of you have ever seen! Holy cow! Holy four-chambered cow stomach! How come your mouths haven't fallen open in shock! Hey, Ken, open your mouth in shock!"

Peter stepped forward. "Maybe it's time to go, Marcus."

"No! My show's not over! I haven't done my most incredible trick yet!" He tried to pull up his sleeves, but then he realized that he was wearing a short-sleeved shirt. "Nothing up my sleeves, right? Right? Right? Right? Right?"

"That's right," Peter said warily. "Nothing up your sleeves."

"And nothing up anybody else's sleeves, right?"

"Uh, we can't really speak to that," said Peter.

"Here's what I'm going to do. I'm going to read everybody's mind! Not just one mind. That would be too easy. Everybody's mind at once!" He began pointing at people. "I'm going to read your mind, and your mind, and your mind, and your mind, and your mind."

Peter grabbed Marcus by the arm, but Marcus shook him off. "Don't touch me! You'll break the spell!"

"You need some alone time," he whispered.

"I need nothing!" Marcus squeezed his eyes closed. "Everybody concentrate on whatever you were thinking about before I started this trick! Concentrate! I can tell you're not all concentrating! Concentrate! Concentrate harder!"

"Uh, Marcus—"

"Concentrate, Peter!"

"It's hard to concentrate with you having a psychotic episode."

Marcus opened his eyes. He could see stars in the corner of his vision. "You were all thinking of...*eight!* The number eight was on all of your minds! Admit it! Admit it!"

Nobody had an expression that said, "Whoa! That's exactly what I was thinking!" They all looked kind of worried.

"Peter, what number were you thinking of?"

"Uh, none. You never asked us to think of a number."

"Chris, how about you?"

"Same here. And if you'd asked me to think of a number, it wouldn't have been eight. It would've been fourteen or something."

"Did anybody think of the number eight?" Marcus asked.

Everybody shook their heads.

"Presto!" said Marcus. "Abracadabra! I successfully named a number that not a single one of you were thinking of! That's far more difficult than guessing a number that you *were* thinking about!"

"I don't think it is," said Chris.

"Do you want to try it?"

"Sure. Forty-seven."

"I was totally thinking of forty-seven," said Marcus.

"No, you weren't."

"What are you going to do? Scoop out my brain and see if there's a forty-seven imprinted on it? My trick was successful. Admit it. Admit that you're awestruck. Admit it."

"Should somebody call the nurse?" asked a kid Marcus didn't know. Or maybe Marcus did know him. He was having difficult recognizing people right now.

"Let's go home, Marcus," said Peter. He looked up at Ken and Chris. "That's okay, right?"

"Yeah, yeah, that's fine," said Ken. "I'm not going to punch him in the middle of a meltdown."

"You're all just scared of my abilities!" said Marcus. "You're scared I'm going to transform you into a monkey! Well, you know what? I might! You're all in danger of becoming monkeys!" He began to point at people. "You're a monkey, and you're a monkey, and you're a monkey, and you were already a monkey and you're a chimp, and—"

All of a sudden, Marcus began to feel self-conscious, as if he were behaving in a manner that might cause his fellow students to stare at him awkwardly.

"Uh, hi," he said. "I would like to apologize to all of you for my behavior just now."

"Apology accepted," said the kid who'd asked if he should call the nurse.

"Sometimes to deal with your problems, you have to let off a little steam. It was not my intention to make anybody uncomfortable or fill any of you with concern for my well-being. I'm okay now. My problems are still there, but I will no longer be pretending that I've turned you into monkeys."

"Disperse," Peter told the crowd.

Marcus crouched down and began to gather his playing cards. He hoped nobody would upload his outburst to YouTube, although at least six or seven kids were likely recording the scene with their phones.

"I'll punch you later," said Ken. "I don't want to do it when you're fragile."

"No, do it at my low moment," said Marcus. "I want to cross it off my list."

Ken shook his head. "Let's just forget the whole thing. I didn't realize you were so bad off."

"How do you know he wasn't faking it?" asked Chris.

"Did you see the crazy look in his eyes?" asked Ken. "You can't fake that." Ken turned to Marcus. "If you need somebody to talk to, give me a call."

"All right. Thanks."

Ken and Chris headed off, and the rest of the spectators went their separate ways. Marcus gathered up both of his decks of cards and shoved them back into his pockets. Each deck was gimmicked in a different way, so he'd have to sort them out later.

"That was interesting," said Peter.

"Did I look undignified?"

"A little."

"At least I wasn't—" Marcus started to say, "Wearing a witch mask," but then he saw some kids within earshot. Peter might go ballistic if his secret identity was revealed, and the school really only needed one student to make a spectacle of himself on any given afternoon.

"I'll give you credit," said Peter. "You're pretty good at keeping bullies from beating you up."

Marcus stood. "Yeah, well, I'm bad at everything else."

"No, you're not. You're great at a lot of things. And I think you're going to do a disappearing shark trick that will make everybody else go as crazy as you just did."

They started to walk home. "I don't know why I told Kimberly that I punched Ken in the face," said Marcus. "That was dumb."

"You told her that?"

"Yeah."

"Why?"

"I just said that I don't know why."

"It could've been worse."

"Yes, I could have told her that I knocked all three of them unconscious with my pinky. The fact that I could've said something worse doesn't mean it was a good thing to say."

"So you exaggerated the story," said Peter. "Big deal. What's she going to do? Never talk to you again?"

"I can't figure out if you're trying to make me feel better or if you're trying to crush my spirit into the dirt."

"The first one."

"You're not a great motivational speaker, Peter."

"I would never say I'm good at talking. What I am good at is seeing when people are beating themselves up and they don't deserve it. I should know. I beat myself up all the time."

"Not to be argumentative," said Marcus, "but you deserve it a little bit."

"For last night, yeah. I'm talking about the past sixteen years."

"Okay, I can't speak to that whole time frame."

"This mess isn't your fault."

"Not to be argumentative again, but I'm actually not

230

blaming myself for this predicament. I'm blaming myself for the sucker punch fib. I can't point fingers at anybody but me for that. But for everything else I'm blaming you, Grandpa Zachary, Sinister Seamus, Bernard, Ken, Chris, and Joe."

"I thought you said you were bad at everything?"

"That's not the same as blaming myself," said Marcus. "And now that I've had a minute or so to recover from my feeling of complete despair, I still think I'm good at some stuff."

"Glad to hear it."

"In fact, I feel a lot better. Maybe that humiliation was exactly what I needed. I'm going to do this trick. I'm going to get a shark no matter what, and we're going to build a tank no matter what. And we're going to make the illusion work no matter what. Sinister Seamus is going to learn that he's messing with the wrong teenage magician!"

"Yeah!" said Peter.

"Who does he think he is, trying to make me live in fear? Threatening me and my family? Changing the rules whenever he feels like it? He's going to wish he'd never heard the name of Marcus Millian III. He's going to wish he'd never broken into Grandpa Zachary's apartment. He's going to wish he'd never been born!"

"Yeah!" Peter said again.

"Maybe I won't go that far. I'm sure he's had some good years that will balance out the bad, so even if he doesn't wish he'd never been born, he'll wish he'd died sooner!"

"Yeah?" Peter said after a moment of hesitation. "I want to chime in, but that's kind of morbid. He's a human being. He had a mother."

"All right," said Marcus. "I withdraw that. But with you as my witness, I'm vowing right now that Sinister Seamus *loses*!"

"Yeah!"

"Hey!" shouted Bernard. Marcus and Peter looked back over their shoulder and saw him chasing after them. "I know you saw me in the parking lot!"

They waited until Bernard caught up with them. He was breathing heavily, even though they hadn't even made it off school grounds yet. He panted for a few moments before speaking.

"Sorry," he said. "I don't run much. I got a gym membership as a birthday present one year, but I never went. I need to get in shape. This is embarrassing."

He panted some more.

"It's okay," said Marcus. "We aren't in a hurry." Marcus hoped Bernard wasn't going to have a heart attack.

"Okay, I'm fine now," said Bernard. He handed Marcus the poster. "Would you care to explain this?"

It was the same poster as before but with a new date.

"Seamus changed the date on me," Marcus explained. "Now we only have—" He looked at the poster and did a quick calculation in his head. "Two weeks?"

"I thought you had a month," said Peter.

"I did have a month! He changed it again!"

"It's almost like he doesn't want you to succeed," said Peter.

"This is unacceptable!" said Marcus. "If he wants to increase the stakes with his evil, murderous ways, fine, but he can't keep changing the time line! That's not how wagers work! You set the rules, and you stick to them!"

"He's Sinister Seamus," said Bernard. "He does what he wants when he wants."

"Well, this is going to backfire. I'm now even more motivated than I was about a minute ago. He wants to change the rules? Let him. It will make his defeat sting even more. Mark my words. This show will end with Sinister Seamus crying on the floor of the restroom!"

"He's got you set for the same day that *Prairie Dogs: A Musical Journey* opens!" said Bernard. "That's my big-ticket show for the season. I can't have people showing up for *Prairie Dogs: A Musical Journey* and make them sit through some belly flop of a magic trick by a fifteen-year-old."

"I won't let you down," said Marcus. "When my illusion is complete, people will feel like they got their money's worth before the opening song of *Prairie Dogs: A Musical Journey* even begins. That I swear!"

"They'll still be putting up the *Prairie Dogs: A Musical Journey* set up until the night before the opening. I can't let you set up the shark tank until that morning."

"That's not a problem," said Marcus, even though it was a pretty big problem.

Bernard sighed. "This is going to ruin me. I wish I'd never said that you only had a career as a birthday party magician."

"I wish that too," said Marcus. "But we're here, and we have to accept the hand we're dealt."

"Is that a card trick reference?"

"No, poker. But you're right. My life needs to be all magic all the time for the next two weeks, so I shouldn't be making poker references. What I meant was that we have to accept the card that our volunteer selected from the deck."

"Unless it's a fake volunteer," said Peter.

"Right."

"And unless you forced the card the person chose," said Peter.

"Right," said Marcus. "What I'm saying is that we can't reverse the chain of events that landed us in this position, and right now I'm *happy* about it because we're going to *win*!"

"I wish we'd been playing some patriotic music during that," said Peter.

"That would've been overkill."

"I could probably download something on my phone if you want to give the speech again."

"Nope. The moment has passed. And we've got work to do!"

23

AS THEY WALKED home, Marcus alternated between feelings of intense confidence and feelings of wanting to throw up. If Peter had been playing "America the Beautiful" on his phone, it would've gone, "*O beautiful for spacious skies* [Retch!], *for amber waves of grain* [Bleargh!], *for purple mountain majesties* [Hurl hurl hurl!] *above* [Retch!] *the* [Retch!] *fruited* [Retch!] *plain* [Bleargh!]."

Still, the feelings of intense confidence made Marcus think that he could really do this. And if it ended up being a crushing defeat, at least he'd go down swinging.

Hmmmm. That was a baseball reference.

Or was that a boxing reference? Marcus wasn't sure. Oh well, it didn't matter. It was supposed to be all magic references from now on.

If it ended up being a crushing defeat, at least the rabbit was out of his hat.

That didn't make any sense, and the entire concept of "at least he'd tried" was flawed. After all, failing at this trick meant his gruesome demise, but still, he was glad to have a more positive outlook on his chances.

They reached Peter's street. "Do you want me to come over and help you?" Peter asked.

"No, but you said you could get me the materials for the tank, right?"

"Yeah."

"And you're not stealing them from any crime lords, right?"

"Right."

"Nobody is going to come after us?"

Peter hesitated.

"Nobody is going to come after us?" Marcus asked again.

"I'll make sure nobody comes after us."

"Do you promise that this glass wasn't meant for hospitals or orphanages or anything?"

"I'm not stealing the glass," said Peter.

"How are you getting it?"

"Maybe you should have plausible deniability."

"This sounds bad."

"It's not bad."

"Is anybody getting hurt?"

"I promise you that if we drew an imaginary line in the air and one side of the line said, 'Moral,' and the other side said, 'Immoral,' we'd stay completely on the 'Moral' side."

"I'm trusting you," said Marcus.

"Your trust isn't misplaced."

"Don't make me regret trusting you."

"You won't."

"I'm already regretting it a little, and you haven't done anything yet."

"You're making the right decision."

"I'm wavering."

"Don't waver."

"And now I'm starting to freak out a little."

"Relax," said Peter.

"I expect zero gangsters to shoot down my door. Zero."

"There will be no gangsters."

"All right," said Marcus. He took out his notebook and opened to the page with the tank diagram. "Take a picture of this so you know exactly what we need."

Peter took a picture with his cell phone. "Got it."

"We'll talk tomorrow."

Peter saluted. "Aye-aye, sir."

Marcus resumed walking home, wondering if he'd just made a terrible, horrible, ghastly, disastrous, apocalypse-starting mistake.

Probably.

Oh well. He had no choice, especially since he only had one good hand right now. It was hard to set up a shark tank if you were screaming in agony every time you picked up a pane of glass.

Now all he needed was the shark. Unfortunately, that had always been the most challenging element of the illusion. Given the tension between him and Kimberly, he couldn't rely on her to get him a shark anymore.

His phone vibrated. It was a text message from Kimberly.

FYI, I have not taken back my promise to help you find a shark.

Really?

I'm waiting to hear back from some people. No guarantees.

That's fantastic! I really appreciate this, Kimberly.

Can I come over after practice?

Of course!!!!!!!!!!!!!!!

Don't get cute with punctuation. I'm still annoyed you lied to me.

Sorry.

See you after practice.

When Marcus got home, he went up to his room and decided to get his homework out of the way first. If he lost the bet, his grades wouldn't matter, but he wanted to behave as if he had a future in life.

He tried to read a chapter in his history book, but the words looked like they were slamming each other in a mosh pit. He was having equal difficulty focusing on his other assignments until he realized that if he squeezed his injured hand, the jolt of pain removed all other thoughts from his mind. If he told anybody about this technique, he suspected that he'd end up in therapy, but for now it seemed to be working.

A few minutes after his homework was done, the doorbell rang. He went downstairs and let Kimberly inside.

"How was practice?" he asked.

"Let's pretend we don't need small talk," said Kimberly.

"Okay, so I should immediately start talking about sharks? Do we have a shark yet? Who'd you call?"

"Sharks are second on the list. We're going to talk about our personal issues first."

"Oh, goody."

"The difference between a punch to the face and a punch to the stomach may not seem like all that big of a deal, but I still feel as if I hungered for you under false pretenses."

"Fair enough."

"What this means, though, is that I can stop feeling like a manipulative hag for kissing somebody I see only as a friend. Your lie and my lack of self-control balance each other out."

"It wasn't really a *lie*."

"Do you want to work through our differences or not?"

"I guess technically it was a lie," Marcus admitted.

"What I'm saying is that we've each got a black mark on our record, and we can scrub them off the board and start from scratch. I don't mean from when we first met a couple of years ago. I mean from when you started telling me the story of your bully encounter."

"Sounds good to me," said Marcus. "Here's what happened. I started doing a card trick, and when Ken was distracted, I punched him in the stomach."

"That's an excellent story," said Kimberly. "I admire your courage, and yet I don't feel like kissing you."

"You're not going to keep saying that, right?"

"Nope. That was the last time. So are we even?"

"Yep."

"I'm not saying it won't still be a little awkward, but I won't have to get all flustered and leave."

"I'm glad we sorted this out," said Marcus. This conversation seemed to be a pretty definitive end to any possible romantic relationship between them, but maybe it was for the best.

No, it wasn't for the best, but he'd get over it. At least they were still friends. Friends were good. Everybody needed friends. Why bother with the complications of a girlfriend when she could be a good old-fashioned friend? Right? Right? Right?

"Ready to talk about sharks?" asked Kimberly.

"Absolutely."

"I got you a shark. For free."

Marcus couldn't believe what he was hearing. "Are you serious?"

"Completely. Now this next part is going to be kind of ironic, considering that we were just talking about stretching the truth. But I'm going to need you to stretch the truth."

"How so?"

"When I was calling around, it's possible that I might have exaggerated the importance that a certain Zachary the Stupendous had upon the world of magic."

"By how much?"

"A lot."

"By, say, 30 percent?"

"I may have said that he was one of the most famous magicians of all time, and that sponsoring his great-grandson's stage debut would generate good publicity that far exceeded the value of transporting the shark."

"Sounds like a lie," Marcus noted.

"I'm calling it an exaggeration for the greater good."

"I can accept that and still sleep at night."

"So when you talk to the very kind gentleman who's going to call you this evening, your job is to *not* indicate that Grandpa Zachary may not have been one of the most famous magicians of all time. And if he mentions anything about Grandpa Zachary's Wikipedia page, which I may or may not have updated, don't correct him."

"Is this guy going to be mad when it's over?" asked Marcus. "Should we be worried about enraging somebody with access to sharks?"

"A little. But that's a problem for another time."

"What kind of shark?"

"I asked for his scariest one."

"Well, thank you! This is incredible!" Marcus felt like Godzilla had stepped off his shoulders and gone off to destroy a different city. He was so grateful that he wanted to give Kimberly a big kiss, but fortunately, his temporary insanity had worn off enough so that he knew that would be a poor choice.

"So you're in good shape," said Kimberly. "You've got a shark and a few weeks to prepare the trick."

"Only two weeks now," said Marcus.

"Did I sleep through something?"

"Circumstances changed. The show got moved up."

"I thought it was going to be almost impossible with the original deadline."

"It was."

"Then why did you let them change it?"

"I didn't have a choice."

"How does that work? Bernard can't just revise the terms of the bet."

"There are other parties involved. That's all I can say."

Kimberly stared at him for a while.

"Did you make a side bet?" she asked.

"Maybe." That wasn't a fib, was it?

"With whom?"

"I can't talk about it." Still the truth.

"How much is the bet for?"

"A significant amount." His life counted as a significant amount, right?

"How much?"

"It's not money. I don't have any of that stuff."

"Please tell me that it's not for your left eye or something like that."

"It's not for my left eye," said Marcus. "When the show is over, I'll tell you everything. For now, I just need you to trust me."

"If I see you after the show and you're missing an eye, I'm going to be really upset."

"My eyeballs are in no danger," said Marcus, desperately hoping that it wasn't a lie.

"All right, I won't pry into your business," said Kimberly. "I'm going to head off now, but if you need help, you know where to find me. Let me know when the shark guy calls."

"Thank you. I can't tell you how much that means to me. Much better than using a shark puppet."

"Were you really at the point where you were going to use a shark puppet?"

"No, but I would've gotten there soon."

"Let me know how the call goes."

As soon as she left, a call from an unknown number came through. He pressed "Accept Call," hoping that this would be the call that saved his life.

24

"HELLO?" HE SAID.

"I'm calling for Marcus Millian III."

"That's me."

"Name's Larry from Larry's Bait and Tackle. I talked to your assistant, Kimberly."

"How are you doing?"

"Can't complain, can't complain. So it's my understanding that you're in the market for a fierce underwater predator?"

"A shark, yes."

"I believe I can accommodate this request, but I need to interrogate you first. First of all, do you plan for any harm to come to the shark?"

"Absolutely not," said Marcus.

"Glad to hear it. That would've been a deal-breaker right off the bat. Many people think that sharks are the devil in fish form, but that's not the case. Your average shark wishes you no ill will. Can you say the same about your average human?"

"I guess not."

"You're darn right you guess not. If you're happily floating in the ocean, a shark isn't going to swim up and try to pop your inflatable raft. It's just not the way they operate. If you get bit by a shark, it's because you were bleeding in their water or because you looked like a seal."

"I have no plans to look like a seal."

"Sharks don't have good vision. Their sense of smell is so much better than ours that we might as well not even have noses, but their eyesight is weak. So if they think you're a seal and eat you, it's an honest mistake."

"Noted," said Marcus. "I'm not sure how much Kimberly explained about what we're going to do, but it won't actually involve anybody getting into the tank where they could be mistaken for a seal."

"I'm told that you'll be using strategic mirror placement to make the shark look as if it has disappeared from our plane of existence."

"Yes."

"Will there be any anti-shark messages in your performance? I can't be part of something that makes the audience see them in an unfavorable light."

"No," said Marcus. "The shark will be held up as a noble, majestic beast."

"Good," said Larry. "Sharks get a bad rap. How many people do you think die every year from shark attacks compared to automobile accidents?"

"I'd guess that a lot more die from car crashes."

"*Ding ding ding!* Give the man a stuffed bear from the wall of prizes! When I share that statistic with some people, they say, 'But Larry, that's only because there are more automobiles in the world than there are sharks,' but that isn't true at all. Obviously, nobody has swum around and counted every shark, but some experts estimate that there could be more than a billion sharks in the world."

"How many cars are there?"

"Just over a billion. So it's about equal."

"I never knew that."

"The thing is that tens of thousands of people die in car accidents every year. Yet an above-average year for shark attacks, you're talking maybe five people dead. Average is four-point-two, but obviously a shark isn't killing a fifth of a person."

"I suppose it could bite off a fifth of a person," said Marcus.

"That's the kind of comment that might cause me to rethink lending you a shark," said Larry.

"I apologize."

"I'm just kidding. Gotta have some fun, right?"

"Absolutely."

"So the number of sharks and the number of cars in the world are just about equal, but did you know that as many as one hundred million sharks are killed every year? That's a lot of dead sharks. That's more sharks than you could pile on the Brooklyn Bridge, I assume. Can you imagine if one hundred million cars were destroyed every year? Consumers would be outraged!"

"What kind of sharks do you have available?" asked Marcus, hoping to change the subject.

"Selection varies. I'm told you're looking for something scary."

"Scary would be great."

"Hammerhead sharks are scary. Not only do they have razor-sharp teeth, but those eyes are strange and unnerving. It's like they're looking at both sides of you at once."

"I'd love to use a hammerhead shark. As long as it doesn't hammer my hand."

"What?"

"Sorry. Inside joke."

"Is somebody listening in on this conversation that would appreciate the inside joke?"

"No. A real hammer fell on my hand, so that's what I was referencing. I didn't expect you to understand it. It's something I should have thought instead of saying out loud."

"Happens to me all the time," said Larry. "I've got a great big scar on my chin that's from saying something I should have just thought."

"Anyway," said Marcus, "I can't even describe how great this is. You're doing me a huge favor."

"Don't mention it. It's an honor to be working with you, and I'm proud of you for continuing your great-grandfather's legacy. He was one of the greatest who ever lived. I remember my father taking me to see him when I was a young boy. We'd go every year on my birthday. Some of my favorite memories."

"He's part of some of my favorite memories too," said Marcus.

"I'm just making that up," said Larry. "I didn't believe your assistant for a second. But making one of my sharks disappear sounds pretty cool, and I assume it'll be okay to hand out some fliers for my business before and after the performance?"

"Oh, sure, sure, absolutely."

"I'm also told that the name of my business will be prominently featured on the sides of the shark tank?"

"Yes, of course."

"And perhaps you could incorporate my website address into your spiel during the trick?"

"Yep."

"And if other magicians come up to you after the trick and ask where you got the shark, you'll give them my name, right?"

"Yes, sir."

"We've got a deal."

~~~~

Marcus had a shark!

He couldn't believe it. One hour ago he'd thought all hope

was lost and that he'd be buried in a shallow grave without even a clever statement on his tombstone. But now he felt like he was embarking on what would become a terrific career path.

All he had to do now was put together the tank.

The very complicated tank.

With only one working hand.

And somebody who thought he was a masked crime fighter.

And a "just friends" assistant with whom it was now awkward to communicate.

And almost no time to test the illusion in the actual venue.

And with three (two?) lurking bullies whose thirst for vengeance seemed to have been quenched but could show up at any time to wreak havoc.

Plus, Sinister Seamus could change the rules again.

And he needed a haircut before the show.

And he had this mild rash on his left knee. No big deal in the grand scheme of things. He was pretty sure they had topical cream in the medicine cabinet that would clear it right up. But it was one more thing to worry about.

Despite these challenges, Marcus had faith in himself. He had faith in his friends. He had faith in Larry from Larry's Bait and Tackle.

This was going to be ridiculously amazing.

~~~

"Those are all different sizes," said Marcus.

Peter glanced at the panes of glass that he had lying out on his front lawn. "Yeah."

"The tank needs to be a rectangle, not a misshapen eleven-sided monstrosity."

"We'll make it work. I've got lots of glue."

＊＊＊

"That's not going to hold," said Marcus.

"It'll hold."

"It already stopped holding."

"Oh, so it did. More glue next time."

＊＊＊

"How's the hinge coming?" asked Peter.

"It's coming just—*ow*!"

"What's wrong?"

"I used my bad hand while you were distracting me."

"Probably shouldn't do that."

"I know!"

"Should I avoid asking questions?"

Marcus shook his head. "You can ask them. I'll accept responsibility for not—*ow*!"

"Maybe we shouldn't talk."

"I just never expected to do this kind of work without using my left hand."

"How's the hinge coming?"

"It's coming fine."

"Really?"

"No."

~~~~~

"So that's going to be the tank?" asked Kimberly.

"It's in the very early stages," said Marcus.

"It'll start to look like a tank eventually," said Peter.

"Hmmmm," said Kimberly.

~~~~~

"It's not looking too bad for a day's work," said Peter.

"We've been working on it for four days."

"I'm just saying that if we'd only been working on it for a day, it wouldn't look too bad."

~~~~~

"It's not looking too bad for six days' work," said Peter.

"We've been working on it for eight," Marcus pointed out.

"Better than it was looking before."

Marcus had to admit that the tank looked like much less of a horrific mess than it did a couple of days ago. Would it come apart when filled with water? He couldn't say with 100 percent certainty that they were going to avoid that particular disaster, but he was feeling more confident.

Kimberly had done an excellent job decorating the bottom and sides of the tank. With the mirror in place—and the mirror had been a *nightmare* to get into place—it almost, kind of, sort of looked like you were seeing the whole tank instead of half.

Of course, "almost, kind of, sort of" wasn't good enough. If the audience said, "Well, we almost couldn't see the obvious mirror that separated the tank into two compartments," Marcus would have to consider the illusion a failure. Hopefully, the water would create enough distortion to hide the mirror.

They opened the hinge in the mirror—the hinge had been a *nightmare* to install too—and looped a garden hose through it. Peter turned on the water, and he, Marcus, and Kimberly stood and waited.

The tank did not collapse as the first drops of water struck the bottom, so that was nice.

As the water level rose to an inch, no streams of water poured from any of the corners, which was also nice.

Two inches.

"This might work," said Marcus.

"Don't jinx it!" said Peter.

"I don't believe in jinxing."

"Well, I do! I believe in it like crazy! Don't say stuff that could end up being ironic!"

"It's not going to hold," said Kimberly.

Peter glared at her. "Don't try to use reverse psychology either. Just watch and let events unfold the way nature intends."

"No, I'm serious. It's not going to hold," said Kimberly.

The entire front pane of glass toppled forward. Fortunately, it landed on the grass. Unfortunately, beneath the grass there was hard dirt that hadn't yet turned to mud from the spilled water, and the glass shattered.

"More glue next time," said Peter.

~~~~~

They watched in silence as the water level rose to a couple of feet.

And then three feet.

And then four feet.

And then four feet.

And then four feet.

"Why isn't the water level rising anymore?" asked Marcus.

"There's a big leak in the back," said Peter. "But at least the tank didn't—sorry. I almost said something ironic."

~~~~~

Marcus, Peter, and Kimberly watched in silence as the water level rose.

Three feet.

Four feet.

And then five feet.

"It's full!" said Marcus. "We did it! We did it!"

Peter shut off the spigot. "We're the greatest magicians ever!"

"Do you hear a cracking sound?" asked Marcus.

"No," said Kimberly.

"Good. Me either."

"How long should we stand here and stare at it before we declare victory?" asked Peter.

"I say we test the trick a couple of times and then drain it," said Marcus. "No reason to tempt fate."

For the practice run, the role of the hammerhead shark was played by a blue towel attached to some fishing line. Marcus dropped the towel through the trapdoor in the mirror and then lowered the trapdoor (which was also attached to fishing line) back into place. You could see the outline if you looked closely, but people in the audience wouldn't have the opportunity to look closely. They would be sitting too far away.

Kimberly draped a black curtain over the tank.

Marcus lifted the trapdoor, pulled the towel through the opening, and dropped the trapdoor.

Kimberly pulled the curtain away.

"Whoa!" said Peter. "That shark disappeared!"

"You work the trapdoor," said Marcus. "I want to watch."

They tried the trick again. Marcus watched as the towel sank to the bottom. Kimberly tossed the curtain over the tank, and when she pulled it away, the towel was gone!

Was it the most spellbinding illusion in the entire history of magic? Nah. Would the audience gasp in astonishment at Marcus's feat of dexterity? Nah. Kimberly and Peter were doing the actual work. Still, it was a pretty cool trick.

"Does anybody else hear a cracking sound?" asked Peter.

"No," said Marcus.

"No," said Kimberly.

Peter pumped his fist in the air. "Woo-hoo!"

25

SHOWTIME WAS AT three o'clock in the afternoon. Marcus woke up at three o'clock in the morning. He didn't need to be up anywhere near this early since Bernard wasn't going to let them into the theater before noon. But his body said, "Wake up! You're nervous!" and he was forced to comply.

He paced around for a while, silently rehearsing his patter.

This could be his last day to not be dead, but he decided not to dwell upon such matters.

He paced and paced and paced and paced and paced and paced and paced and paced and paced and paced. Once he was done, he paced and paced and paced and paced and paced and paced and paced and paced. With that process complete, he paced some more.

Mom made a huge breakfast that Marcus was too queasy to

eat. "You're going to do wonderfully," she said. "We're really proud of you."

"Thanks," said Marcus, trying to choke down the corner of a piece of toast.

"This is the first of many shows to come," said Dad. "So remember that the stakes are low."

"I will."

After he ate some breakfast, sent a text to check in with Kimberly, and spent some more quality time pacing, Marcus and his parents went over to Peter's house, where a U-Haul truck was waiting in the driveway. When Marcus rang the doorbell, Peter's mom answered the door. He'd never seen her awake and off the couch.

"You must be Marcus!" she said. There were dark circles under her eyes, but she looked freshly showered and happy. "Peter's said so much about you! I'm sorry for what happened to your hand."

"It's okay," said Marcus, flexing his fingers. "It doesn't hurt anymore."

"That's wonderful," she said. "He can be so clumsy."

"Yeah."

"Give me a hug." As Marcus gave her a hug, Peter's mom whispered into his ear, "Thank you for not revealing his secret identity."

Together, Marcus, his parents, Peter, and Peter's mom very, very carefully loaded the tank into the U-Haul. They got it into the vehicle without dropping it, sparing them the need for a *wah wah wah waaahhhh* musical cue.

Then Marcus and his parents returned home. It was time to get ready.

He put on his black suit and adjusted his tie. As Marcus checked himself out in the mirror, he had to say that yep, he looked like a magician.

He practiced his patter once more.

It was going to go fine. He knew it was going to go fine. It was definitely going to go fine. He was pretty sure it was going to go fine.

He gave Mom and Dad a hug. They were driving separately, and he'd see them at the theater in fifteen minutes. But it felt like the right moment to give them a hug to thank them for all of their support. And soon he might be too nervous to use his arms.

He rode to the Pinther Theater in the U-Haul with Peter and his mother. Apparently, they could tell that Marcus was nervous beyond the ability to form words with his mouth because neither of them spoke.

When they arrived, Bernard opened the rear stage door for them, and the team very, very carefully unloaded the tank and moved it to the center of the stage. The set for *Prairie Dog: A Musical Journey* was a bright desert landscape, which didn't match the dark look Marcus would have preferred, but there was nothing he could do about it.

"That doesn't look very sturdy," said Bernard.

"It'll be fine," Marcus promised.

"May I pound on it to be sure?"

"Please don't."

Bernard sighed. "I don't know if this means anything coming from me, but I hope you impress everybody. I don't even care about losing my honor to Zachary. I'm rooting for you."

"Thank you."

Marcus attached his garden hose to an outside spigot and then draped the other end over the side of the tank and began to fill it. He was confident that the tank would hold, though he hoped that Bernard had plenty of towels just in case. Peter and the others seemed to realize that he still wasn't in a talking mood, so they left him alone to fill the tank.

A man in a prairie dog costume walked over to him. "You Marcus the Stupendous?"

"Yes."

"You'd better not steal my thunder, kid."

"It's just a quick trick."

"You're lucky I went for this. I could've shut down the trick. Bernard owes me ten thousand dollars, so he's in no position to tell me I have to have an opening act. Don't think you're getting a cut of the ticket sales."

"I don't want any of the proceeds," said Marcus.

"When we start singing 'Popping Our Heads Out of the

Dry Tan Ground,' I expect the audience to be fully engaged. I don't want to look out there and see people talking about your pet shark. Got it?"

"I'll make sure the trick sucks."

"I mean it. I'll bite you. The teeth on this costume are foam rubber, but my real teeth will break the skin." The man in the prairie dog costume pointed to his googly eyes and then pointed at Marcus to indicate that he'd be watching him. Then he left.

When the tank was about half full, a man in shorts and a green polo shirt approached the stage. "You the magician?"

"Yes."

The man extended his hand. "I'm Larry from Larry's Bait and Tackle."

"Hi! Great to meet you!"

Larry tapped the glass. "This where the shark is going?"

"Yes."

"You ready for it?"

"Yes. Do you need somebody to help you wheel in the aquarium?"

Larry shook his head. "Nope. I've got it in a plastic bag. Be right back."

Marcus didn't think it was safe to carry a hammerhead shark in a plastic bag, but he wasn't the expert.

A few minutes later, Larry returned holding a very small plastic bag filled with water.

"What's that?" Marcus asked.

"This is your shark."

"It's a goldfish!"

"It's a young one, I'll grant you that, but this here is a certified hammerhead shark."

"But…but…but…it's head isn't even shaped right!"

"Hammerheads aren't born like that," said Larry. "They're born with normal fish heads, but as they mature, their heads expand into the hammer shape that we associate with this type of beast. Its scales will also gradually change from the gold color that you see here to a more sharklike hue."

"You were supposed to bring me a full-grown shark!"

"I don't recall that being part of the agreement."

Marcus poked at the bag. "That's a goldfish! You brought me a goldfish! I can't do the amazing, disappearing shark illusion with a goldfish!"

Larry peered at the bag more closely. "Now that you mention it, there are certain goldfish-like qualities to its appearance."

"What am I supposed to do now?"

"Laugh."

"What?"

"You're supposed to laugh."

"Huh?"

"I was having a bit of fun with you. This is a goldfish. Once I bring in the shark, there's an element of peril involved, so I always try to lighten the mood with a good goldfish joke."

"Oh."

"Sometimes I use a minnow."

"You get that I almost passed out, right?"

"And if you had, I'd know that you lacked the nerves of steel required to be this close to a man-eating hammerhead shark. I know I said on the phone that shark attacks are rare, but it's something I say to help myself sleep at night."

"Could you please go get the shark?"

"Sure. I'll be right back…as long as I don't lose a hand."

Larry walked off the stage, chuckling.

Marcus did deep breathing exercises for about fifteen seconds before Kimberly walked into the auditorium. She looked stunning in a sparkly red dress.

"Wow," said Marcus. "Best magician's-assistant-who-does-more-work-than-the-actual-magician ever!"

"Thank you." She made her way to the stage, moving slowly in high heels. "Stop being so nervous."

"How do you know I'm nervous?"

"You're ghost-white and drenched with sweat."

"That's a good clue. Yeah, basically, I'm so nervous that I could burst into tears at any second. If that's the kind of thing you'd like to witness, stick around."

"I'm confident that you won't cry," said Kimberly. "This is your big moment. Enjoy it."

"I'll try."

"Here we go," said Larry, wheeling in a small tank. "One hammerhead shark for the magician."

Marcus hurried over to look into the tank. The shark was about three feet long. Small by hammerhead shark standards, but unmistakably a real shark. If Marcus accidentally fell into the tank with it, he'd go absolutely berserk with terror, which was exactly the kind of shark he wanted.

"Perfect!" Marcus said.

"His name is Frenzy," said Larry. "He mostly eats sewer rats."

"I didn't bring any of those."

"It's okay. Fish guts will work just fine."

"I brought plenty of those."

"All right, you get to know Frenzy for a moment while I go get the net." Larry winked and left.

"He looks like a cold-blooded killing machine," said Kimberly.

"Yep."

"When I gaze into his eyes, I see no soul."

"Nope."

"I don't want to turn my back on him."

"You can turn your back. It's fine."

"I'm hypnotized by his evil."

"He's not evil," said Marcus. "Believe me, I've seen evil, and it's not in shark form."

The shark looked directly at Marcus with the eye on the left side. It seemed to be saying that it would cheerfully devour his arm all the way up to the shoulder, though Marcus supposed he could be misinterpreting the message.

Marcus and Kimberly kept a close watch on Frenzy until Larry returned with a net that seemed too small to safely transport the shark from one tank to the other.

"Gonna need your help with this," Larry told Marcus.

"I'd rather not."

"And I'd rather not get woken up every morning by the guy in the upstairs apartment practicing in his homemade bowling alley. We can't always get what we want. C'mon, let's do this."

Marcus and Larry both gripped the net by the handle.

"Don't let go," said Larry. "We mess this up, we've got a hungry shark flopping around on the floor by our feet."

Kimberly stepped off the stage.

Marcus and Larry dunked the net into the water. It took several tries, but they finally caught Frenzy. They quickly lifted him into the air and into the other tank.

"I'm glad that worked," said Larry. "I didn't want to say anything, but I noticed while we were lifting him that I'd brought the net with the big tear in it."

"Is that another joke?" asked Marcus.

"I wish it had been," said Larry. "I wish it had been."

"So let's test his hunger," said Marcus, going around to the back of the tank. He lowered the trapdoor. "First, we have to get him to swim down into the bottom half."

"To do that, the food would have to sink down there before he can eat it," said Larry. "I don't know about that. He's pretty fast."

"Can we put the food on the end of a stick?"

"Oh, he'll eat the stick before it gets down there."

"Well, we need him to swim through the hole."

"Then you've got quite a challenge to… Oh, look, there he goes."

Marcus pulled on the fishing line, closing the trapdoor.

"Frenzy looks angry," said Kimberly.

Marcus opened a small cooler that rested on the floor behind the tank and removed a fish gut. (At least he'd been told they were fish guts. In theory, they could be any kind of guts.) He dropped it into the tank and then opened the trapdoor.

Frenzy immediately swam through the hole and ate the red blob.

It worked! Marcus wanted to scream with joy.

"Nice job," said Larry, wheeling the smaller tank off-stage. "If you don't mind, I'm going to place a flyer on each seat before people start coming in."

Kimberly hurried up on stage and gave Marcus a big hug. "It's going to work! Nothing can go wrong!"

"Plenty can go wrong," said Sinister Seamus. Marcus hadn't even noticed that he was sitting in the center seat of the front row. He grinned the most evil grin Marcus had ever seen. "*Plenty*. But don't let that worry you."

26

THE CURTAIN WAS closed.

The theater was full.

Marcus was queasy.

Peter was in place behind the tank and hopefully would stay invisible to the audience even after the black cloth was pulled away. Kimberly stood next to Marcus on the stage, waiting for their cue. They could hear Bernard welcoming the audience and telling them about the other fine upcoming productions at Pinther Theater, such as *Hamlet* and *Ned's Pimple*.

"You're going to do great," Kimberly whispered.

A simple response to her comment like saying, "Thanks," or, "Uh-huh," or just nodding his head seemed warranted. Marcus couldn't do any of that though.

He tried to assure himself that he'd be fine. All he had to do was talk. He talked literally every day. Ever since acquiring the power of speech as a toddler, he couldn't think of two consecutive days in which he hadn't spoken. The trick was going to go beautifully, and it would be his first big step to becoming a professional magician.

"And now," said Bernard, "before we get to the part you're here to see, please bear with us as we present…Marcus the Stupendous!"

The stage curtains opened.

Marcus stood there, microphone in his hand, staring out into the crowd. It was too dark to see any individual faces, but he imagined the audience as one big face, staring unhappily at him.

Introduce yourself, said his brain.

His mouth said nothing.

He wanted to lift his hand to wipe the sweat off his forehead, but he couldn't even do that. He was completely paralyzed. He was doomed to stand there until some stagehand took pity on him and closed the curtain again.

He was able to move his eyeballs enough to glance at Kimberly, who was trying to signal with her own eyeballs that it was time to begin.

Somebody in the audience coughed.

At that moment Sinister Seamus coming after him with a knife didn't seem so bad. No, he had to do this. He'd put too much work into this trick to let the whole adventure end with him standing there looking stupid. It wasn't fair to his grandpa, Peter, Kimberly, or even the cast and crew of *Prairie Dogs: A Musical Journey*.

"Hello," he said, pleased that he was able to pronounce both syllables. "I'm Marcus Millian the third, but you can call me…Zachary the Stupendous!"

Wait, had he just introduced himself as Zachary? That was embarrassing.

"I mean, Marcus the Amazing," he corrected.

"I mean, Marcus the Stupendous," he corrected again.

"I am a man of many identities," he told the audience. "It changes from moment to moment."

The audience tittered.

That was a pretty decent ad-lib. Maybe he'd incorporate it into future performances.

"With me is my lovely assistant, Kimberly," he continued, pointing to her with a sweeping gesture. She curtseyed to the crowd.

After saying a couple dozen words in front of the audience, Marcus felt some of the tension ease from his body. Several of his lines had been wrong, but still, he was up on stage, successfully speaking, and nobody had booed him. He wasn't nearly as nervous as he'd been before the curtain opened. He could definitely do this!

"Sharks," he said, gaining confidence. "They are fierce predators. And excluding a couple larger species, none is more dangerous than the hammerhead."

With dramatic flourish, Marcus tugged off the curtain over the tank, revealing Frenzy. The audience did not let out a huge collective gasp as he had anticipated, but somebody near the front of the theater exclaimed, "Oh, cool!"

"Hammerhead sharks are man-eaters," said Marcus. "I'm taking my own life into my hands by standing up here, and you're taking your lives into your hands by sitting so close to a tank that may not meet federal regulations."

The audience chuckled. Marcus hadn't meant it to be a joke. He wasn't kidding.

"Over the years, magicians have made many things disappear," said Marcus. "Coins. Cards. An elephant. Their careers." He paused for laughter. When there wasn't any, he cleared his throat and continued, "But unless my Google search was incorrect, few of them have ever tried to make a shark vanish."

Marcus was doing fine. He might go so far as to say that he was enjoying himself. Why had he been so worried about this performance? It had been a waste of perfectly good stomachaches.

"And today, before you delight in the musical adventures of a family of prairie dogs whose natural habitat is about to be bulldozed, I will make Frenzy the Hammerhead Shark, disappear!

"Now you see him…"

He and Kimberly picked up the cloth with a flourish and

draped it over the tank. Marcus stepped off to the side so he could watch Peter.

That was Peter's cue to pull the chain that would release the hinge. Peter pulled the chain and then frowned. He held out the chain for Marcus to see. "It snapped!" he whispered.

Marcus didn't want the audience to see him whispering back, so he settled for using his eyes to convey sheer panic.

"I have to reach in there," Peter whispered, not sounding thrilled by the idea.

Marcus was supposed to tell the audience, "Now you don't!" but he probably needed to stall, to talk about something else to fill the silence. "Did you know that there are about the same number of sharks in the world as there are automobiles?" he asked.

Marcus glanced out of the corner of his eyes again. Peter looked like he was psyching himself up. He took a deep breath, closed his eyes, and slowly reached for the shark tank. Then he opened his eyes again, as if realizing that he should probably look before he reached into a shark tank. Peter reached through the hole. He tugged on the hinge, and it flopped open. Then he yanked his hand out of the tank so quickly that Marcus was worried the audience might hear water splash onto the stage.

"Almost nobody ever gets eaten by a shark," Marcus informed the audience. "But for those who do, it's a pretty bad way to go."

Peter tossed some fish guts through the hole.

Marcus wished Peter could quit moving around so much because he could hear the water dripping.

No, wait. Was the water was dripping from the bottom of the tank?

That could be problematic.

"He's not going for it," Peter whispered.

Had they fed him too much in the test? Was Frenzy full?

Marcus lowered the microphone. "Add some more," Marcus whispered through clenched teeth, trying to keep his lips frozen like a ventriloquist.

Peter added some more guts.

Marcus knew he shouldn't keep peeking behind the tank because the audience would find it very suspicious. This was all taking way too long. He was going to have to accept that there was an excellent chance that the patrons of Pinther Theater would think that his magic trick sucked.

He glanced over to the other side of the stage. Bernard stood in the wings, arms folded angrily over his chest.

"He won't swim for the guts!" Peter whispered. "I don't know what to do!"

Marcus thought he heard a cracking sound, but it may have been the sound of his mind preparing to explode.

Kimberly looked concerned. She was probably thinking about the thousands of places she'd rather be than standing on stage while a magic trick did a complete belly flop. She might even prefer to be in the tank.

"Now you see him," Marcus repeated, even though the audience couldn't see the shark since they had covered the tank a good two or three minutes earlier. To Marcus, though, it felt like two or three hours.

"I'm out of guts!" Peter whispered.

Marcus wasn't sure what to do. Should he just apologize to everyone? "Sorry, ladies and gentlemen," he could say. "My bad. Because of technical difficulties, I'll be feeding myself to Frenzy now."

Maybe he should just run for it.

He couldn't see the people in the audience, but he could sense them fidgeting. An illusion was quite a bit less beguiling when there was a curtain draped over the tank for eighty-three hours. This was supposed to happen quickly. They could've lifted the shark out and transferred him to another tank by now.

"Shake it around," Kimberly whispered, also speaking without moving her lips.

Peter reached into the tank, grabbed a gut, and shook it.

"Ladies and gentlemen," said Marcus, "I'd like to apologize…"

"He's through!" said Peter.

"…for blowing your mind!"

"But I can't close the hinge!"

"Just reach in there and close it!"

"He's on my side now!"

Marcus wanted Peter to just do it, but he couldn't in good

conscience order him to reach into bloody water when there was a hungry, man-eating shark swimming around. He didn't want to make a bad show worse by having Peter lose some fingers.

Inspiration struck Marcus. If he did this trick again, he'd leave the curtain off and show the audience how the magic was done. He'd put a fake hand on Peter that was hooked up to some tubes that pumped cherry juice, and make it look like the shark bit off his hand. That's what he should've done this time. That would've been awesome.

Kimberly hurried around to the back of the tank, reached through the hole, pulled the panel back into place, wiped her wet hand on the curtain, and then returned to her spot.

Wow.

She looked like she was going to keel over from fright, but she'd done it!

Marcus was so stunned that it took him a moment before he remembered the audience.

"Now you don't!"

Marcus and Kimberly pulled off the curtain with a dramatic flourish, revealing the "empty" shark tank.

The audience offered up some halfhearted, sympathetic applause. Even if they didn't know how the trick had been done, the slow pacing had pretty much wiped out any sense of wonder and amazement.

Marcus grinned.

It worked! Eventually. With more time to rehearse and perfect the illusion, Marcus's vanishing shark trick still had potential. As angry as Sinister Seamus had been about the revelation of the secret to all magic, it really *was* practice. Marcus would get it right the next time.

And he now knew that he could overcome his stage fright.

And that Peter and Kimberly were incredible friends who were dedicated to him and the show enough to put their hands in a shark tank.

If Seamus didn't kill him, Marcus was confident that he, Peter, and Kimberly could put on an *amazing* performance next time.

"Well, that was mildly interesting," said Bernard, stepping out onto the stage. "Give us a moment to clean up, and then we'll begin *Prairie Dogs: A Musical Journey.*"

Somebody in the front row center stood and applauded. It was a slow, loud clap. It didn't surprise Marcus at all when the clapper eased toward the light of the stage and turned out to be Seamus. He turned around and addressed the audience.

"So," said Seamus, "what did you think of Marcus the Stupendous?"

Some people in the audience clapped politely, probably because they didn't think there was any reason to be jerks to a fifteen-year-old. Somebody said, "Eh." There was some enthusiastic clapping from the back row, which he assumed was his family.

"Did any of you believe that he made a shark disappear?" asked Seamus.

The audience made various noncommittal noises.

"Anybody?" asked Seamus. "Raise your hand if you did."

One man in the second row raised his hand.

Seamus pointed to him. "You bought into the illusion?"

"Well, I mean, I'm looking at the tank right now, and there's no shark in it. Obviously, while the curtain was over the tank, they had some shark wranglers sneak behind it and carry the fish off-stage. But the shark disappeared, so in answer to your question, yeah."

"Anybody else?" asked Seamus.

Mom and Dad, who'd gotten terrible seats in the back row because they didn't have a seasonal subscription to the Pinther Theater, raised their hands. Seamus ignored them. He looked over at Marcus and smiled a wicked smile.

"I'm sorry, young man, but I must consider your trick a failure."

27

MARCUS'S HEART RACED. Surely, Seamus wasn't going to walk on stage and slash at him with his knife-wand in front of everyone. That would be crazy. Of course, Seamus was extremely crazy. Still, even *he* couldn't reach *that* height of craziness…could he?

"I've done many bad things in my life," Seamus told the audience. "I've lied, stolen, and yes, taken some human lives. I used to be proud of that. I'm not anymore. There was a time not so very long ago that I'd brag about being evil. I wore my reprehensible personality like a badge of honor. Every time I tossed a handful of ladybugs into a blender to make a smoothie that I didn't even bother to drink, I'd giggle. But I don't want to be Sinister Seamus anymore. I want to be Snuggly Seamus."

The cracking sound from the tank grew louder. Marcus

hoped that Seamus would wrap up his little speech soon so they could drain it. Otherwise, something very inconvenient might happen.

"I've received some bad news from the doctor," said Seamus. "It turns out I'm unlikely to live more than fifteen, twenty years tops. It's the kind of news that causes a man to look back and reevaluate his life. I'll be honest. If this trick didn't work, my original plan was to murder Marcus and his entire family. But I've discovered that I don't *want* to murder Marcus and his entire family. I don't even want to murder Marcus. I don't want to murder anybody."

"Thanks," said Marcus.

Snuggly Seamus turned to him. "Congratulations, Marcus Millian III. The illusion wasn't insanely spectacular, but your great-grandfather would've been proud of you anyway. You have a long, prosperous career ahead of you as a magician."

The front pane of glass popped completely off. As the water poured forth, the rest of the glass and mirrors crashed to the floor.

At least 90 percent of the people in the audience screamed as Frenzy the shark was swept forward right off the stage and onto Seamus. The old man shrieked as the shark thrashed and snapped at him.

Peter, now exposed to the audience, quickly bent down and started picking up pieces of the tank as if he planned to hurriedly reconstruct it.

"Get it off me! Get it off me! Get it off me! Get it off me! Get it off me!" Seamus shouted.

Larry rushed out from backstage. "Don't hurt my shark! I'm coming for you, baby doll!"

"Ladies and gentlemen, this all part of the show!" Marcus assured everyone as he leapt off the stage. He might not like Seamus, but he couldn't stand around and let him get eaten. Grandpa Zachary would have expected more from him.

Most of the audience members in the front row had stood up and scattered away from the flood of water. Nobody was currently assisting Seamus, either because they believed Marcus when he said this was part of the show or because most people, given the option, typically elected not to go near a carnivorous shark.

Larry leapt off the stage next to Marcus. "Do you want to take the head or tail?" Larry asked.

"Tail please."

The hammerhead chomped down on Seamus's shoulder. Seamus expressed loud displeasure.

"Oh, uh," said Larry. "I can only handle seeing fish blood." His eyes rolled to the top of his head, and he passed out.

"Get it off me! Get it off me! Get it off me! Get it off me! Get it off me!" Seamus repeated.

Marcus tried to grab the fierce predator's tail, but it was thrashing too much for him to get a hold of it. Peter and Kimberly jumped off the stage to help. Then they sort of stopped and looked at each other as if hoping the other would take the initiative.

Marcus now understood why most magicians opted to make bunnies disappear.

"Don't let me die this way!" Seamus wailed. "It's memorable but undignified!"

Peter had apparently lost at rock-paper-scissors to Kimberly, so he knelt down next to Marcus and also grabbed for the shark's tail. He got a grip on it and tugged. But his hands slid off the fin, and he tumbled onto the floor.

"Start the show!" Bernard shouted. "Start it!"

"There's broken glass on the stage!" one of the guys in prairie dog costume said.

"You've got padding on your feet! Just do it!"

Peter grabbed for the shark's tail again. As he tugged, Marcus decided that he had no choice but to pry its jaws from Seamus's shoulder. He grabbed each side of its hammer-shaped head, tried not to squeak in terror, and pulled as hard as he could.

The shark's jaws came free.

Kimberly hurried up the three steps onto the stage and then ran backstage. Three prairie dogs stepped into the spotlight. Music began to play.

"*We are the prairie dogs,*" they sang. "*We're not cows, and we're not hogs. Nor are we slimy frogs. We are the prairie dogs.*"

Marcus and Peter hoisted the shark away from Seamus. It

was a lot heavier than Marcus expected. In fact, he didn't think he was going to be able to hold it, which would be a pretty big problem if he dropped an aggravated shark with a mouth filled with razor-sharp teeth onto his leg.

"We live on the prairie. Where everything is merry. And all of us are hairy. Right here on the prairie."

The audience seemed very confused. Marcus noticed that his parents along with Peter's mother were rushing forward, so he waved them away. "All part of the show!"

Marcus and Peter carried the shark away. Its mouth was wide open, ready to devour the nearest appendage, and Marcus knew he had a whole new inspiration for his nightmares.

He'd thought Kimberly had run off in cowardice, but then he saw her rush back onto the stage, holding the net. Oh, yeah. The net. That was way smarter than carrying the shark with their bare hands.

"We've got holes in the dirt. We never wear a shirt. Nor do we wear a skirt. We've got holes in the dirt."

Marcus desperately clung to the shark's head as gently as he could. Even if he didn't drop it onto his foot, he didn't want to hurt the poor shark, which was only following its genetic nature. Dropping the shark on the floor would be cruel, and nobody would be entertained then.

"You're losing your grip!" Peter warned.

"I know!"

"Don't lose it!"

Kimberly lowered the net under the shark. Marcus and Peter gently released the shark in the net, hoping it wouldn't wriggle free and go after an innocent audience member.

"*We eat grass and some bugs. By which we don't mean slugs. We mean bugs that aren't slugs. And we're big fans of hugs.*"

Marcus was starting to wonder if *Prairie Dogs: A Musical Journey* was actually worse than his illusion. He'd assumed that Bernard upheld pretty high-quality standards at the Pinther Theater, but he was starting to reconsider that idea.

Peter took the handle of the net from Kimberly and lifted Frenzy. It was obviously a challenge for him to carry the writhing beast, but he got up the stairs onto the stage without dropping it.

Marcus turned his attention to Seamus, who was now standing on his feet again. His suit, which had been very crisp a few minutes ago, was no longer appropriate for classy events. Marcus had seen plenty of unhappy people in his life, but on a rage scale of one to ten, ten being the most enraged, Seamus was an eight thousand. (It was not a scientifically accurate scale.)

"Stop the music!" Seamus shouted.

The music lowered but didn't stop. The prairie dogs continued dancing around the stage, taking care to avoid the broken glass.

Seamus pointed at Marcus with his good arm. "You ruined my chance at redemption."

"Sorry," said Marcus. "But let's be honest. Making one decent speech doesn't excuse you for a lifetime of evil."

"I spent nearly twenty minutes refining that speech."

"Did you really get bad news from the doctor?"

"That's irrelevant."

"It's kind of relevant."

Seamus turned to the orchestra pit. "Can you *please* stop the music? We're trying to have a conversation here!"

"The show must go on!" Bernard bellowed from the wings.

The prairie dogs, who were doing a dance with multi-colored umbrellas, ignored Seamus. After all, Bernard paid their salaries.

"So are you still trying to redeem yourself?" Marcus asked.

"No," said Seamus. "I most certainly am not."

"Bummer," said Marcus.

"And now I take my leave!" Seamus reached into his inside jacket pocket, felt around a bit, and frowned.

"What's wrong?" Marcus asked.

"I was supposed to throw down a capsule so I could disappear in a puff of smoke, but I think the shark ate it." Seamus sighed. "What a dud of a day."

Peter and Kimberly walked back onto the stage. "Frenzy's back in his original tank," Kimberly announced. "He seems to be doing fine."

"Excuse me," said the prairie dog Marcus had spoken with earlier, "but we're trying to put on a musical performance here."

"I apologize," said Kimberly.

Seamus reached into his jacket again and took out his pistol. As he pointed it at Marcus, a few people gasped.

"This isn't part of the show!" said Marcus. "I know you were told to put your cell phones away, but somebody please call the police!"

"It *is* all part of the show," said Seamus. "Marcus the Stupendous will now perform the legendary bullet-catching trick!"

"None of this is scripted!" Marcus insisted. "I'm in legitimate danger! Please take this seriously!"

"He's going to catch the bullet between his teeth and give you all a great big grin," said Seamus. "Get ready to take your final bow, Marcus!"

"What's that in your head, Seamus?" Marcus asked.

"Huh?"

Marcus gestured at him, and a stream of cards shot through the air, just as they'd done when he'd done the trick with the little kid who'd started this whole mess.

Fifty-two cards struck Seamus in the face. They weren't particularly heavy cards, and they weren't sharp or anything. But Seamus had just been attacked by a hammerhead shark, and he wasn't in the best physical condition. He dropped the gun and fell to the floor.

"Do you want me to sit on him until the police get here?" Peter asked.

"That would be nice," said Marcus.

Peter sat on Seamus.

Kimberly gave Marcus a hug.

The prairie dogs kept singing.

Larry remained unconscious on the floor.

Bernard shook his head and looked like he wanted to cry.

Some people in the audience applauded while the rest acted very, very confused.

28

"I THINK I'M going to retire the disappearing shark trick," Marcus said on Monday afternoon as he stood outside of the school building with Kimberly and Peter.

"Is it because Larry's Bait and Tackle threatened to sue you?" asked Kimberly.

"That's part of it."

"Not everything was perfect," said Peter. "Especially the part where the tank came apart. That was less than perfect. I wish that hadn't happened. I can't remember what point I was trying to make."

"Were you trying to be inspirational?" Marcus asked.

"Um, I don't think so."

"Then I have no idea what you were going to say. But I've proven to myself that I can stand up on stage without freezing or babbling like an idiot. With more time to prepare and practice, I know deep in my heart that I can be a successful magician."

Reviews of the magic show had been mixed. The local paper called it "glorious chaos," while an online reviewer called it "a baffling mess." Everybody agreed that *Prairie Dogs: A Musical Journey* was "the feel-good musical of the year! An absolute delight! You'll leave the theater humming and dancing!"

Sinister Seamus was in jail. Presumably, since he was so old, his evil deeds would keep him behind bars for the rest of his life. Would he escape and return seeking vengeance? Marcus didn't know. Marcus would not be inclined to return to seek vengeance if *he'd* been chewed up by a hammerhead shark, but he wasn't Sinister Seamus. He'd have to be careful.

Marcus pointed at Peter. "With your help, we're going to design bigger and better tricks. And more vigorously test them for safety."

"I'm in!"

Marcus pointed at Kimberly. "And I want you to be my assistant when we perform these bigger and better tricks."

"Actually, I've been inspired," Kimberly said. "I'm going to be a magician."

"Really?"

"Yes. Want to be my assistant?"

"Sure," said Marcus. "We could trade. I'll assist you in your show, and you can assist me in mine." It would be great! They could be magicians together!

"No, I was kidding," said Kimberly. "I'm going to be an architect. But I'll be your assistant until we graduate high school."

"Thanks." Oh well. Marcus was glad that she could joke with him again. She might not be his girlfriend, but they could still be friends.

"I've decided that I no longer need to be the Witch," said Peter.

"What's the Witch?" asked Kimberly.

"You don't want to know," said Marcus.

"Yes, I do. I feel like I'm missing something."

"You are, but it's something that you should miss."

"I wore a witch mask and fought crime," said Peter. "But I have another source of fulfillment in my life, so I'm going to donate my mask to a kid who wants to be a witch next year for Halloween."

"That's very kind of you."

Peter looked at Marcus. "And while we're sharing, I have to confess that I got all the tank supplies from my cousin. I wanted you to think that I stole them from criminals even though I kept insisting that I hadn't, but it was just my cousin. He's pretty mad that he won't get the glass back."

"I see," said Marcus. "Anything else?"

"My mom said she was really proud of me for the way I handled the mechanical shark, and I never corrected her."

"Well, that's between you and her."

"Yeah, I just figured I'd throw it out there."

"Anyway," said Marcus, "I'm banned from the Pinther Theater for the rest of my life, my children's lives, my grandchildren's lives, and my great-grandchildren's lives, but I'm sure there are other places we can put on a show when we're ready."

"What about birthday parties?" asked Peter.

"Sure, why not? I'll perform anywhere I can."

"Hey!" somebody shouted.

Marcus, Kimberly, and Peter glanced over. It was Ken, flanked by Chris and Joe. They walked over, scowling.

Peter stepped forward. "I think you need to just walk on by."

"Why?"

"Because I'm not letting you bully me anymore. Or my friends."

"Oh, we're not here to bully anybody. We were scowling before. But that's because there was a pop quiz in eighth period, and we weren't paying attention in class."

"Then what do you want?"

"I hear you guys beat up a shark," said Ken.

"Sort of," said Marcus.

"Sort of is close enough for me. That's awesome. I've never met anybody who tackled a shark before." He extended his hand to Marcus. "You're all right in my book, Magic Boy."

Marcus shook his hand. "Thanks."

"If you need anything, let me know. I mean, not money, but favors or stuff."

"I will."

Ken, Chris, and Joe left.

"I've got to go to chorus," said Kimberly. "But I'll text you tonight."

"Talk to you then," said Marcus.

"I've got to go too," said Peter.

"Where?"

"I joined chess club. I'll probably be terrible at it, but I won't know until I try. I figured that an extracurricular activity would be good for me, and they needed an extra person."

"Okay. Well, have fun."

"I will."

Peter and Kimberly left.

Marcus began to walk home. Would Grandpa Zachary be proud? He probably would have called it "an unfortunate but necessary first step on the road to success." It hadn't been the world's greatest magic trick by any stretch of the imagination, but his parents had been proud. Marcus had been proud of himself and his team, and he was pretty sure that Grandpa Zachary, the infamous Zachary the Stupendous, would've been proud too.

He smiled as he walked home, already planning his next trick.

ACKNOWLEDGMENTS

Thanks to Donna Fitzpatrick, Lynne Hansen, Michael McBride, Jim Morey, Annette Pollert-Morgan, and Rhonda Rettig for their magical help with this book.

ABOUT THE AUTHOR

Jeff Strand has loved magic all his life, but he can't even shuffle a deck of cards properly, much less do a trick of his own. That's why he's an author instead of a magician. He's written a bunch of other books, including *The Greatest Zombie Movie Ever*, *I Have a Bad Feeling about This*, and *A Bad Day for Voodoo*. He lives in Florida, where everything is magical—or at least weird. Check out his website at jeffstrand.com.